Berkshire

Edited By Donna Samworth

First published in Great Britain in 2018 by:

 Young**Writers**

Young Writers
Remus House
Coltsfoot Drive
Peterborough
PE2 9BF
Telephone: 01733 890066
Website: www.youngwriters.co.uk

FOREWORD

Young Writers was created in 1991 with the express purpose of promoting and encouraging creative writing. Each competition we create is tailored to the relevant age group, hopefully giving each child the inspiration and incentive to create their own piece of work, whether it's a poem or a short story. We truly believe that seeing their work in print gives pupils a sense of achievement and pride in their work and themselves.

Every day children bring their toys to life, creating fantastic worlds and exciting adventures, using nothing more than the power of their imagination. What better subject then for primary school pupils to write about, capturing these ideas in a mini saga – a story of just 100 words. With so few words to work with, these young writers have really had to consider their words carefully, honing their writing skills so that every word counts towards creating a complete story.

Within these pages you will find stories about toys coming to life when we're not looking and tales of peril when toys go missing or get lost! Some young writers went even further into the idea of play and imagination, and you may find magical lands or fantastic adventures as they explore their creativity. Each one showcases the talent of these budding new writers as they learn the skills of writing, and we hope you are as entertained by them as we are.

CONTENTS

Emily Johnson (10)	52
Harrison Ord (11)	53
Henry Britler	54
Matthew Sandles	55
Jack Bartholomew (9)	56
Emily Georgina Long (10)	57
William Hennah (9)	58
Emily Eaves (9)	59
Noah Smith (10)	60
Holly Kitching (10)	61
Matilda Burchett (10)	62
Lauren Amelia Hatt (10)	63
Cydney Amelie Owen (10)	64
Rebecca P (9)	65
Pierre Denis (9)	66
Charlotte Anne Carpenter (10)	67
Curtis Haines (9)	68
George Edward Keylock (9)	69
Samuel Donegan (10)	70
Cameron Young (11)	71
Esme Baron (10)	72
Eloise Gale (10)	73
Scarlet Thompson (9)	74
Jessica Smith (10)	75
Clara Phillips (10)	76
Lauren Brown (10)	77
Caitlin Hunt (11)	78
Hannah Haines (10)	79
Arthur Pienaar (11)	80
Morgan Galgey (10)	81
John-Paul Perry (10)	82
Louis Richard Lovelock (10)	83
Hayden Harriss (9)	84
Dylan Bacchus (9)	85
Tane Newton-Cook (10)	86
Matthew Whatley (10)	87
Owen Humphreys (10)	88

St Gabriel's School, Sandleford Priory

Elsy Williams (10)	89
Millie Jones (10)	90
Evie Dancer-Bown (10)	91

Imogen Brown (10)	92
Eloise Taylor (10)	93
Eleanor Bayford (9)	94
Madeleine Herd (10)	95
Zoe Toms (9)	96
Nerea Halley Martin (11)	97
Ella Newborough (10)	98
Olivia Cole (10)	99
Ava Elverson (10)	100
Katie-Rose Verney (10)	101
Neve Wright (9)	102
Grace Lewis (10)	103
Ellie Abbot (9)	104
Grace Cunliffe (10)	105
Josephine Margaret Keen (11)	106
Olivia Emily Violet (11)	107
Sofia Abel (10)	108
Charlotte Hamilton (11)	109
Elspeth Mary Coughlan (9)	110
Zara Taylor (9)	111
Ismay Gallup (10)	112
Maddie Goss (10)	113
Gabby Thorne (10)	114
Mia Wright (9)	115
Charlotte Bedford (10)	116
Georgia Wilson (10)	117

St Paul's Catholic Primary School, Tilehurst

Thomas Colin Phillips (9)	118
Daniel Sanchez Pereyra Iraola (8)	119
Patrick McCoy (8)	120
Lottie Mae Stretton (9)	121
Charley Pearson (8)	122
Tom Carroll (8)	123
Michal Nowicki (9)	124
Thomas Jakes (8)	125
Jayden Soloye (8)	126

St Peter's CE Middle School, Old Windsor

Tristan Meller (11)	127
Joseph Rodgers (11)	128
Kumayle Hussain (11)	129
Camran Gangarh (11)	130
Arjun Singh Kharay (10)	131
Eleanor Rose Terry (10)	132
George John Williams (11)	133
Charlotte Roberts (10)	134
Ayesha Scott (10)	135
Nihal Bath (10)	136
Georgia Harradine Quarteman (10)	137
Isaac Gadsby-Gower (10)	138
Lauren Tullett (10)	139
Thomas Butler (10)	140
Angel Richards (10)	141
Thomas Mullan-Smith (11)	142
Maham Omar Mirza (10)	143
Jack Hollick (10)	144
Jaye Long (11)	145
Eisha Darcia (10)	146
Freya Holden-MacDonald (11)	147
Charlie McCreanor (10)	148
Finnley Viotto (10)	149
Poppy Jane Alden (10)	150
Rebecca Barrack (11)	151
Ellie-Mae Brazier (10)	152
Evie Lewis (10)	153
Archie Padwick (10)	154
Marcus Barron Cheeseman (10)	155
Simone Williams (10)	156
Max Kaczmarczyk (10)	157
Jason Finlayson (10)	158
Ben Corrigan (10)	159
Ethan Wood (10)	160
Scarlett Breach (10)	161
Millie Edwards (10)	162
Hannah Rowley (11)	163
Jasjotika Singh (10)	164
Riley Moule-Wood (11)	165
Hannah Evans (10)	166

Adam Elliott (10)	167
Jessica Tambling (10)	168
Olivia Rigby (11)	169
Holly Alden (10)	170
Alaina Howard (11)	171
Harvey Keegan (11)	172
Eve Jarvis (10)	173
Amanda Kyla Valenzuela (10)	174
Grace Bennett (11)	175
Charlie Field (10)	176
Danny Dick (10)	177
Sara Renata Espinosa (10)	178
Jessica Davies (10)	179
Zaki Sfendla (10)	180
Ryan Wood (10)	181
Jerusha Jayasingh (10)	182
Billy Palin (10)	183
Ethan Lee (10)	184

Thorngrove School, Highclere

Charlie Fogg (9)	185
Gus Murray (10)	186
Chloe Shore (9)	187
Setareh Elvinna Garett (9)	188
Eleni Gomez (9)	189

Waverley School, Finchampstead

Qiu Qiu Wei (9)	190
Margaret Samuella Oppong-Mensah (9)	191
Olivia Woolger (9)	192
Keira Di Rocco (9)	193

THE MINI SAGAS

Bunny's Birthday

"Today is the perfect day to bake a carrot cake for Bunny's birthday," announced Toy Kitty. (The children were away.)

Smiling happily, Toy Puppy volunteered to assist Kitty. Grabbing the ingredients, she realised there were no carrots left.

At once, she whizzed off like a speeding bullet to the giant fridge.

Moments later, Kitty arrived with the carrots and they began their task. As evening approached, the scrumptious cake was ready and the party kicked off.

Suddenly, the children returned home. Astonished at the sight of the cake, the hungry children gobbled it up.

"Oh dear!" exclaimed Kitty.

Inaya Prakash (8)

Dotty And Me

In a dark town, there lived a small boy named Joshua and a rainbow-coloured teddy called Dotty. Now Joshua had a secret, he had a magic bracelet. If Josh said, "Come to life," Dotty would come alive. Dotty's favourite adventure was when Josh decided to make a time machine. They went to his garage to find bits for his machine. They built the incredible machine in five hours.
Dotty and Josh went to have tea with Queen Victoria and cake with Marie Antoinette but then they had to go home. It was such an adventure!

Joshua David Samuel Rowe (8)

Where Am I?

Where am I? The last thing I remember, I was joined together by a sticky substance called glue. Now, I am in this vast, tenebrous room! It is moving forward and suddenly stopping. Argh! What was that noise? *Honk! Honk!* The wall of the room just fell apart.

I am falling... falling into this plastic bag? Where am I now? Outside a shop window, people are staring at me! What's going on? I'm lost! Where am I?

Ishmal Abbasi (11)

Make-Up Disaster

"Sorry Barbie, I've got to go now," explained
Liv. *Stomp, stomp, stomp,* went the shoes.
"We're free," shouted Barbie as the door slammed
shut.
Whizzzz! came the car. "Here's your lift Ma'am."
"Just getting my make-up." Barbie sashayed to the
car, throwing her arms up, yelling, "Woohoo."
They stopped in the sister's room, Barbie jumped
out, put the make-up down and relaxed on the
multicoloured eyeshadow. After a while, the car
came back into the room and *bang* went the make-
up.
The toys froze as the sister rushed in shouting,
"Livvv." The colourful make-up had exploded
everywhere!

Carys Deller-Law (11)
Hemdean House School, Caversham

A Midnight Feast

"I'm starving!" moaned the doll.

"Let's find some food," whispered the teddy. So they crept down the stairs and found a truckload of food.

That night the two friends tiptoed to the place where they found the food. Soon, there was munching and slurping. "Mmm, yummy," sighed the doll.

"Yes and I found it," said the teddy.

"No, I did," replied the doll. Soon they started arguing and didn't hear the footsteps.

A giant human opened the door. "What's that?" exclaimed Emily, surprised to see her favourite toys near her marvellous dinner! "How peculiar and strange!" she said.

Saanvi Kaipa (10)
Hemdean House School, Caversham

Zog And The Escape

There was once a girl called Hannah and she had a toy alligator called Zog.
They were at Alice's house and Alice said,
"Let's play in the paddling pool." Zog and Teddy (Alice's toys) got put on the slide. They fell in! Then they got put on the radiator and Alice and Hannah went off.
Zog then decided to jump out of the window!
Teddy shouted, "No!" but Zog was already climbing out.
Then Hannah and Alice came in. They saw Zog out of the window. Hannah ran outside and grabbed Zog. The escape wasn't as easy as planned!

Hannah Hodgson (11)
Hemdean House School, Caversham

The Toy Disco!

It's morning, all the humans are tucked up in bed. *Poof!* Mr Giraffe is awake, he stumbles onto the sofa. "I'm so lonely, I wish I had company." Suddenly Mr Giraffe has an idea. "I know, I'll go to Toys 'R' Us, I'm sure I will have company. "I'll start packing now!"

Mr Giraffe sets off. The street is empty and quiet, nobody notices him slip out. "Just a few more steps, I'll be there." *Tap, tap, tap.* "Yes, there it is!"

He runs as fast as lightning. *Whoosh!* He is there. "Finally, I will never be alone ever again!"

Hana Khan (9)
Hilltop First School, Windsor

Alien And Ghosts

Tik. The lights went off. "All clear," said Ghost.
"Let's go!" exclaimed Alien. Everyone came to the fort.

The war began. *Bang, pow, clang, bash...* It was a violent war. It went on forever and ever and ever. The UFOs went on flying. The ghost tanks went on the battlefield. They went *bang! Clash! Pow! Bash!* They went down to 30, 29, one by one, they went down. Then the ghost tanks fired and some aliens dropped off the roof.

Tik. The lights went on. Now it was a real battle. "Everyone fire."

"Ouch!" Everyone ran!

Tyler Kumar Tamang (8)
Hilltop First School, Windsor

Fluffy's Big Adventure

"Ooooh, will she pick me?" Fluffy whispered from the shelf she was hidden on.

"No, just give up," sighed an old Barbie doll.

"They don't see us here, well unless they bother to look," Fluffy sighed.

A lady walked towards them. Fluffy got picked!

"You'll make a great gift for Lilybell!" the lady happily said.

"Mummy, I love it!" a little voice said.

Fluffy looked around, where was she? It was moving like a big car. *Owww*, Fluffy thought. She looked up. "Awwww!" she quietly said. She was being hugged by a cute little girl.

Poppy Fletcher
Hilltop First School, Windsor

Run Tikáh, Run!

Tikáh had the sting of a scorpion, the head of a falcon and the wings of an eagle. He was a dragon.

One night he told his friends, "I'm going to escape now, anybody with me?"

"You get all the holidays, I don't," protested Reindeer.

"I don't care," argued Tikáh.

They carried on for five minutes until Cly said, "Stop..." They both stopped, they knew Cly could eat anything.

"Yaaaaa!" Tikáh screamed and jumped onto Rascal who ran to his catflap and ran into the dark. Tikáh stopped, thought, then ran back to his room.

Joshua Weller (8)
Hilltop First School, Windsor

Minion

Once, a Minion got taken from the supermarket. He got bought by a boy. He left him in the garden because he played with him. He said, "Freedom!" The Minion was running with relief but then he saw somebody, it was Traction Man! "Who goes there?" he snapped. Traction Man saw the Minion. "Are you a monster?" he shouted.

"No," the Minion yelled, but Traction Man didn't believe him.

He said, "I don't believe you."

"I don't mean you any harm," said the Minion but Traction Man started to fight. He broke him.

Krishan Patel
Hilltop First School, Windsor

The Soldiers

"Hello, hello, all clear," said Archy, "let's go, let's go, come on."

Tap, tap, creak! They looked behind themselves, no one was there. "Phew!" said Archy.

"Let's carry on," whispered Josh, Archy's friend.

Tap, tap, it carried on until they met Pirate Pete... They all froze and Oliver was just about to step on the toys but he stepped on the floor and Pirate Pete caught Archy.

Archy and the army were able to jump out of his ship and run away. Pete caught up but... Oliver came. They all got stomped on!

Ibraheem Yasir Baig (8)
Hilltop First School, Windsor

Max And The Desert

"As a cowboy, I shall go to a desert." So Max found a sandpit. "Yes, I need to find shelter before it's night."
He found a cottage for shelter and went to bed.
"Mum, I'm hungry, I need to find food!" said Max, but no animals were in the desert. "So, so hungry. I'm gonna find food, yes."
He went to find food but how could he in a desert?
"I've found a cow! Time to lasso it."
"Moo," said the cow.
"Yahoo," shouted Max. "Pull, pull, I did it. Yahoo."
Nom, nom, nom. He ate it.

Reece Jonah Blake (8)
Hilltop First School, Windsor

The Enchanted Island

Creak! This is my chance to escape. *Creak!* goes the window as I jump out, *poof!*
The parachute is up and 3, 2, 1, I land. For some reason, I'm on an island.
As I step further, "Growl!" Out pounded a big, cuddly tiger onto me. Soon, more animals. After a while, hundreds of animals were cuddling me, then thousands, then millions.
Then I realise that the animals are toys! After that, I start cuddling them myself.
That night, I sleep with the tiger I met during the day. Then I have a big party.

Soleil Willow Rose Rembges (8)
Hilltop First School, Windsor

The Enchanted Woods

"It's clear. Come on, let's go," said Monkmonk.

"Let's go," whispered Fluffy.

"Here we are," whispered Monkmonk.

"Nothing's here," said Fluffy.

"You are wrong, Fluffy," shouted Monkmonk. "It's Caxel," shouted Monkmonk.

"He's gone, let's go," screeched Fluffy. "We're lost," cried Fluffy.

"Just keep going," said Monkmonk.

"Why has it gone bright?" screeched Fluffy.

"It's the exit," said Monkmonk.

Aizel Atif
Hilltop First School, Windsor

Millie Vannilie

"Argh!" shouted Millie Vannilie from Amelia's bag. Amelia had just come out of school and was running to the park with her friends (as usual, this was Millie's least favourite ride of the day). "Oh no," screamed Millie.

She fell out the bag along with a few pencils. Of course, Amelia didn't realise that her bag suddenly got lighter, because it was bobbing up and down non-stop.

Soon, Amelia was just a blob in the distance. Millie was on her own. Beside her, there was a tree. Millie paced around the tree. She heard a voice. It was Amelia!

Sofia Davenport Bishop (9)
Hilltop First School, Windsor

The Story Of The Found Money

"Oh the coast is clear, let's come to life. Hello, who are you?"

"Hi, I'm Miss Rabbit Piggy Bank, I have lost my money."

"How?"

"Well, I fell off the shelf and no one knew but now I've lost it all."

"Let's go and find your money. It might be under there or over here or on here or maybe there."

"Yes, here it is I've found my money!"

Suddenly, Laila came in. "Argh!" Everyone screamed but luckily she did not notice and that was the story of the lost money!

Laila Elizabeth Purba (7)
Hilltop First School, Windsor

Time To Groove

"Go, go, go." The elephants shot across the sky with silver wrapping paper to turn the light into a sparkling new disco ball.

Robo stared at the disco ball. Robo was terrified of going on stage but he had to do it, so he closed his eyes and started to dance.

He was the best dancer but he slipped and lost a battery. "Aahh!" The crowd gasped.

An army person shot a screw. A limited edition baseball bat fell. *Bang!* and hit the ground and flipped the battery in the air which landed in the back of him. "Yes! Woohoo!"

Dexter Colin Mitchell (9)

Hilltop First School, Windsor

Flopsly Out Of Bed!

In the morning Flopsly fell out of the bed and said, "Oh seriously, I have to get back on my owner's bed." She hopped and calmly said, "Where are my friends, the toys?" Then she grumbled, "Ohooo." Then Ava, her owner, came in, she trod on Flopsly. Flopsly tried to keep it in but then she screamed, "Ow."

Suddenly, Ava said, "What's that?" And then whispered, "Hello." No one answered. Ava looked everywhere, even in the toilet.

While Ava was away Flopsly went to the bed and slept.

Ava Gurung-Poudel

Hilltop First School, Windsor

Rex Gets Mad

Roar! roared Rex the toy dinosaur. He was mad that Jack left him because he didn't like Rex anymore.

Actually, Jack went camping. Troll said to Rex, "Jack went camping." But Rex felt rejected. Rex was blaming every toy. He blamed Troll, Nom Num and more.

Then Rex fell asleep and took a break. When he woke up, he blamed more toys. He shouted, "Hey, you're the one who made Jack go away!"

But the toy he blamed was Little Mac and Little Mac screamed, "I didn't," and Rex burst into tears with a boohoo!

Ved Patel
Hilltop First School, Windsor

Pink Fluffy Unicorn

One day, I was actually bought! I was in Toys 'R' Us and they gave me so much attention. It was like a Jacuzzi with rose petals!

Sadly I was bought by Pink. She was the meanest and leanest girl in the world. I got squeezed in bed, shoved in the car and thrown in the turkey salad! Then I was stretched in the car by Pink. 'Pink fluffy unicorn,' she repeated.

"Stop it," Mum said.

The next day, she threw me into the deep, dark ocean. 'Help, my feathers are getting wet. Please, someone, help me!'

Aarya Shahir
Hilltop First School, Windsor

Dolly

I want to get out of this place! I need to push this door open. That was hard! *Thud!* I just jumped down the step. That was tiring.

I need some water. I'm gonna get out my baby bottle. *Slurp!* How am I going to get down all these stairs?

I'm sitting on the step, I hope I don't fall off. *Kaboom!* I fell off! But it's OK, I did this amazing trick. Shall I do that for the rest of the way? I will.

This is going to be an interesting trip... I nearly got squashed. That was close!

Luke Stanford
Hilltop First School, Windsor

The Adventure Of Pikachu

Pikachu came to life! He walked across the room silently. The kid said, "Where is that noise coming from?" After that, Pikachu got thrown in the stinky, dark bin. He quickly got out and was free.

One night, Pikachu once again came to life, at midnight! The kid was snoring loudly and didn't hear anything. Pikachu went to the kitchen and ate some chocolate.

All of a sudden, the kid's mum came. Once again he went in the stinky, dark bin. The rubbish people came and Pikachu lived in the bin forever!

Joshua Erema (8)
Hilltop First School, Windsor

The Teddy Hunt

It was the middle of the night. Mickey Mouse crept out of bed. I was asleep, then I noticed something. Mickey had gone. I crept out of bed, got the keys to the car, and strangely drove off quite well!
I looked all around town, but I couldn't find him anywhere! So I drove back home and crept back upstairs to bed.
It was morning and I went downstairs. I looked in the shed, the kitchen, the sitting room and upstairs again, but I couldn't find him. Then I looked in all three of the drawers and, "Yeah!" got him!

Zakareeya Bouqdour
Hilltop First School, Windsor

Buddy The Bear

Izzy is playing with a bear. A boy walks past and says, "That's Buddy and I want to play with him." A teacher walks past and takes the bear and puts it in the cupboard. Buddy jumps out and watches TV with his friends from the cupboard.

Then a teacher comes to make coffee but she sees the toys have moved. "How did they get there?" she mutters.

She then leaves and goes outside. "Phew, close call," said Buddy.

"Yeah, we totally need to be careful next time!" says Robo Bat.

Nusrat Ahmed (9)

Hilltop First School, Windsor

Pinkie Pie's Great Escape

One dark night, I was fast asleep when Pinkie Pie clambered all over me to get on the floor. "Pinkie Pie, can we play I spy?"

"Sure," screamed Pinkie Pie.

"Shhh," blurted out Sweetie Pie.

"Let's play," whispered Felicity, "I spy."

"Wait," said Sweetie Pie.

"Everybody hide," everybody screamed.

"What's that?" I said.

"She's gone," snapped Pinkie Pie.

"Let's go," muttered everybody.

Thea Shields (9)

Hilltop First School, Windsor

Emojis

In the evening, Pillow Emojis rolled out of bed and started arguing. "No, I'm sleeping with Rachel!" Devil snapped.

"No, I am," cried Sadness.

"Huhm," smiled Smiley.

"Oh," mumbled Poo.

Then Anger ran like a bull and Devil flew out the window.

Rachel skipped into the room. "Where's Devil?" she exclaimed. "Oh, there you are. How did you get there?" Rachel ran downstairs. "I'm sleeping with you."

Jasmine Akrasi (9)
Hilltop First School, Windsor

Pikachu And The Xbox 360

Now's my chance, thought Pikachu as his owner drifted off to sleep. Pikachu jumped up and pulled the door handle down. The door flung open. Pikachu tiptoed through the hall and down the stairs and into the living room. Pikachu walked to the kitchen and made himself a cup of tea. Then he settled down on the couch, sipped his tea and played Minecraft on the Xbox 360!
In the morning, Pikachu's owner found him sitting on the couch playing on the Xbox 360!

Zayn Hussain
Hilltop First School, Windsor

Robby's Big Game

"Robby, I found you," mumbled Uni. Then Robby found a coin.

"Yes!" he screamed.

Then Bad Piggy came in. "Oi, I want to play hide-and-seek."

Everyone snapped, "No!"

But Robby barked, "Yes of course."

I then woke up from my dream. Robby muttered, "Phew." They continued hide-and-seek while I went to sleep again. But before I got tucked up, I found out that my teddies were in the wrong place!

Faith Thomas
Hilltop First School, Windsor

The Adventures Of Emojis

One night, a Poo Emoji had a plan to escape the attic. He found a Dude Emoji. He told the Dude Emoji the plan. He liked the plan.

Then it was morning... "Oh no," said Poo Emoji, "What are we going to do now?"

"I know," said Dude Emoji, "let's climb out of the window."

"Good idea. Let's go!" They climbed the wall to get to the window and then they got out!

Oliver Broadbent (8)
Hilltop First School, Windsor

The Battle Of Life

"Sergeant, I've covered the whole place like you told me to," murmured soldier one. The booby traps descended so you couldn't see the carpet. "Men, it's time to go, keep an eye out," exclaimed Sergeant Flargent.

The owner was fast asleep and it was time to do our business. We protected our girl from any harm since she had broken her leg. Her name was Danielle.

Suddenly, Danielle fell out of bed. It was very dangerous. "Ouch!"

"Is she going to be OK Doctor?"

"Sergeant Flargent, is that you?"

"Yes, who are you!"

"Nurse Polly."

"Nurse Polly!"

Erin Grand (10)
Jennett's Park CE Primary School, Bracknell

The Magic Twist

One scorching afternoon, two friends, Jude and Jamie, bought themselves a new magic box from Toys 'R' Us. They began by playing with the deck of cards, trying to learn some spectacular tricks. Minutes later, their friends knocked at the door. They left the cards on the floor and rushed outside to play.

Several hours later, they returned home to find the Joker cards were now blank, leaving only a J in the corner. Puzzled and confused, they bent down to inspect the blank cards. Immediately, the cards consumed their bodies.

Later that evening the mother walked in to find...

Archie James (9)
Jennett's Park CE Primary School, Bracknell

The Princess And The Unicorn

"I wish I was a real princess!" whispered ragged doll Lucy. The sun was rising and her wish came true. Lucy always wondered what was behind the magic door. She took a deep breath and stepped through.

She saw unicorns, adult ones and baby ones learning how to fly. One of the pink unicorns flew down next to her. "Would you like a ride?"

Lucy didn't hesitate. She jumped on her back and they flew and flew until Lucy saw from high above all other toys frozen.

She felt sad, the unicorn landed on a toy shelf leaving Lucy there.

Bozena Anne Jaasi (9)

Jennett's Park CE Primary School, Bracknell

The Legend Of The Toy Stealer

One normal day, an eight-year-old girl called Jessie was playing with her favourite toy mermaid.
A few days later it was Jessie's ninth birthday and her main present was a new phone! As days passed, the poor mermaid was forgotten about.
As night fell on that very same day, an evil dream was lurking from house to house, searching for forgotten toys to take to his lair so the children would forget about them.
As soon as he arrived, the mermaid was taken! He was seen by her friends so they set off to find her...

Katie Page (10)
Jennett's Park CE Primary School, Bracknell

The Magic Garden

One day, a boy named Elliot walked down the street. He saw a beautiful garden. Every day, he kept stopping at the garden to check on the flowers.

One day, when Elliot walked down the street, the flowers were all dead. Then Elliot realised the special gem was missing. This gem kept all of the wonderful flowers colourful.

Elliot remembered that when he was little, he was given a special gem. Elliot put the gem in the special pot.

All of the colours came back and Elliot decided to buy the garden.

Danielle Dickinson (10)

Jennett's Park CE Primary School, Bracknell

Tiger Gets Them Again!

"Someone's coming!" whispered Bear. He scampered up onto a nearby radiator and was ready to pounce on who he thought was Tiger, his old arch-enemy.

Bear's old friend, Lion, opened the door. The brown, four-legged creature leapt onto poor Lion's mane. They both screamed in surprise and looked at each other with astonishment.

Tiger was on top of the wardrobe; he began to cry with laughter. "Hah! Tricked you again you fools. I'm the only demon in this household and I'll always get my way!" he sneered at the two friends and chuckled quietly under his breath.

Anna Piercey (10)
Oldfield Primary School, Maidenhead

The Invasion Of The Talent Dolls

"I will never join you," shrieked Ann.

"You have no choice!" cackled the grinning doll. She was covered in a midnight-black ninja suit. Ann began to run, aiming to get out the house. From nowhere, a small black leg appeared and tripped her up.

The doll began to chant, "Show your true talent, join us now and help evil dolls take over the world." Ann felt herself shrinking. Her room rose around her and a whirlwind of clothes surrounded her. By the time the ninja had finished her chant, Ann had a bow and arrows slung around her back.

Isabelle Gorf (10)
Oldfield Primary School, Maidenhead

Fridge Fiasco

"It's cold in here!" said Pippa Polar Bear.

"Yes, freezing!" moaned Patrick Polar Bear. Toy time was almost up and the Polars would be plastic soon.

"What's that?" asked Mum.

"Ice cream!" exclaimed Patrick.

"I'm hungry Mum," said Pippa.

"Alright, climb in," said Mum.

The Polars clambered into the pot. They licked the vanilla victory when suddenly, a net was thrown over the pot. "Ha, I knew my toys were alive!" came a girl's voice. "Don't worry little toys, I won't hurt you, my name's Claire, and I'm your owner!" The Polars were scared but also relieved they were rescued!

Eleanor Lyles (9)

Parsons Down Junior School, Thatcham

The Twin Armies

Slowly, the tidal wave of pawns attacked, swarming the battlefield and infiltrating the Black Army.

The knights gallantly charged forwards, slashing enemies to the ground while their valiant, noble stallions whinnied in rage. One... two white pawns fell to the might of the opposing queen. However, many more black warriors succumbed to the force of the white rooks and bishops.

Eventually, all black combatants had fallen, aside from the king. A few warriors moved.

"Checkmate," Sam grinned slyly at Jack while moving his rook to E3.

"Good game!" replied Jack, shaking his friend's hand firmly before helping him tidy up.

Lewis Ching (10)

Parsons Down Junior School, Thatcham

Astroblocks' Army

"I'm fed up with fellow blocks being taken," moaned Astroblocks. Their army was slowly decreasing set by set. They would never rule the shop like this.

There, sat on the shelf, in the distance, was Barbie with her plastic hammer. "We need to get the blocks quickly." Astroblocks dashed round every house in town, then back to Toys 'R' Us. "That was quicker than I thought," said Astroblocks, surprised. "Army attack!"

Barbie was scared and cowered backwards. She didn't fight and gave into Astroblocks, he became ruler of Toys 'R' Us and Barbie was banished to a little human girl.

Isaac Borer (11)

Parsons Down Junior School, Thatcham

The Cheese Moon Adventure

On Planet Zhoogle lived Jeremy the giraffopus and his twin brother Ralph the octoraffe. Jeremy wanted to fly to the moon, Ralph wanted to visit Mars. Queen Carly was undecided on where to go. Queen Carly was stuck. Ralph wanted to make it easier. "Let's battle!" yelled Ralph. Jeremy agreed, he knew he had competition.

Jeremy pushed Ralph off a cliff. "Argh!" he screeched. Whilst Ralph fell to his death, Jeremy heard something and gasped. It was Ralph on a jetpack.

Then they flew to the cheese moon. After eating the delicious moon a crazy, evil species took over the world!

Lois Parker (10)
Parsons Down Junior School, Thatcham

Pirate Attack

As the sun dipped down towards the horizon, the silhouette of the mysterious ship crept into view. While the hours slouched by until dawn, the unidentified ship got closer until the lookout in the crow's nest bellowed, "Pirates!"

The fear in my stomach grew as I recognised the emblems on their sails. It was Captain Cutthroat, the deadliest pirate of the seven seas.

Soon we were in firing range. Death was at our doorstep. The cannon windows flew open. Captain Cutthroat lit the cannons. *Bang, bang, bang.* It was Ali's mum bashing on the bathroom door saying, "Time's up."

Alastair Hughes (11)

Parsons Down Junior School, Thatcham

Spy Teddies: The Lost Toy

"Finally we are here," said Scooby-Doo.

"It's good to go and see our grandpa Rex," replied Tessy Bear.

Ding-dong.

"Tessy Bear, Scooby-Doo," roared Rex the sabre-tooth tiger. "Quick, come in. What seems to be the problem?"

"Well, a robot and his getaway car have kidnapped Mallard and we need Spy Teddies to find him before Isaac wakes up."

"No problem. Spy Teddies, to Atlantis."

Once all the toys were on Atlantis, they set off to find Mallard around the house. After one hour of searching, they found Mallard swimming in the bath!

Isaac Mitcham (10)

Parsons Down Junior School, Thatcham

Georgie's First Christmas

Once, there was a beautiful girl called Poppy who had a very special toy dog called Georgie. Georgie would talk to the other toys when Poppy was gone. Poppy's mum said she had to get rid of some toys as Christmas was coming. Poppy's mum said, "Let's sell George on eBay."

"No!" cried Poppy. "I love Georgie, he's my favourite."

"But you have Kookoo, said Mum, "I thought he was your favourite."

Poppy cried, "I love them both and don't want to get rid of either of them. They are best friends." At that moment Poppy saw Georgie smile!

Paige Wooderson (10)

Parsons Down Junior School, Thatcham

Escape

Abbey pushed through the group. "The area is clear," everyone sighed. "We don't have time, come on."

The group stayed close, making it through the aisle. Abbey whispered, "It's the putty aisle," but it was too late. "Run! Putty attack." Everyone stopped, putty was surrounding them. Out of nowhere, a Lego bridge formed, we crossed it before the putty reached us.

We ran over the Lego bridge, it dismantled when we reached the door. The door opened, light blinding us.

Before we could run, a giant hand came from the light, it grabbed Abbey... Into the light, she went.

Abi Grogan (11)
Parsons Down Junior School, Thatcham

My Diary - Baby Dino

21st November

I'm Baby Dino, I live with Lauren and Alex.
"Everybody loves Baby Dino!" Lauren exclaimed as she and Alex fought!
I can't stand fighting so I run off. I'm lost, I hate it in LA!
Finally, I've found Moose's favourite dog park. I'm hiding in a bush and watching for Lauren to come.

22nd November

I'm still in the park, wait, Lauren's there with Moose! I'm going to hop out in front of Lauren!
We're back home now and Alex is taking me to daycare because it was his fault I was lost. We're leaving now, bye.

Elizabeth Bird (11)

Parsons Down Junior School, Thatcham

The Doll

Bang, bang, bang. A young girl named Lucy listened closely. Loud noises were coming from her bedroom, she ran upstairs and peeped around the corner.

She saw a small doll under her bed. "Hello," whispered the doll, "I'm Petra."

"Hi, I'm Lucy," said Lucy in a scared voice.

"Don't be scared, why are you scared?" Petra's voice got louder.

"Come into the light," said Lucy with scared eyes.

As soon as Lucy saw Petra, she ran downstairs and told her mum, but when they got there, Petra was gone. From then on, Lucy slept with one eye open.

Ripley Freya Johnson (9)

Parsons Down Junior School, Thatcham

The Big Fight

I was in my room, playing with my two favourite toys, Furby and Unicorn. We were playing 'run away from the monster'. The monster was the Furby chasing the unicorn. My mum called me for dinner. "Darling, come down please."
Suddenly, when I left the room, my toys came to life... Furby and Unicorn were fighting about who's my favourite toy.
They used their powers against each other. "I'm her favourite toy!" shouted Furby, then all of a sudden, Minion took the batteries out of Furby. I strolled back upstairs.
"My room's a terrible mess!" I shouted.

Kemi Angcao (10)
Parsons Down Junior School, Thatcham

Barbie's Cake Disaster

"Come on Chloe. If you want to go shopping, we need to go," called Mum. The front door slammed shut.

"Is the coast clear?" whispered Barbie.

"All clear. Operation Party is on!"

With their owner gone, it was time to prepare for the party. The dolls sneaked out from the stuffy toybox and made their way down the stairs.

In the kitchen, they set to work getting flour, eggs, butter and milk to make a cake.

There was mess everywhere like an explosion had gone off. "Quick, someone's coming! Hide!"

"Where has all this mess come from?" screamed Mum.

Mia Cook (9)
Parsons Down Junior School, Thatcham

Revenge

Beep! went the car as Jake approached his driveway. He knocked on the door and his mum let him in. He raced upstairs and started reading his new book called 'Underworld'.

Five minutes later... *Slam!* Jake closed his book and went to check on his mum, but when he opened his door he fell 630,000 miles into the Underworld and landed on solid rock.

A dark figure loomed over him... "Sumo!" he exclaimed. Sumo was his old toy, but his cat had ripped him apart and Jake had to chuck Sumo away. "I'm dreaming," said Jake. It came for revenge!

Jamie McCavish (10)

Parsons Down Junior School, Thatcham

Santa's Adventure

He studied the black tiled floor, stretching out ahead of him. "How am I going to get across this? I need to get to my sleigh so I can deliver my presents."

Santa cautiously stepped onto the first tile - it dropped suddenly. He fell to his knees, an ominous snake-like 'W' stared back at him. Shaking, he stood up and continued his bumpy journey, eventually reaching his target. The gifts would be delivered on time!

The wall to his left suddenly lit up with a mysterious message. Lego Santa jumped in surprise. "What could 'qwertyuiop' mean?" he asked himself slowly.

Dakota Martha Rose Lewry (10)

Parsons Down Junior School, Thatcham

Elephant Mayhem!

The rattle of the rainbow springs released the door whilst the elephants were asleep. A damaged elephant called Rowan heard sudden movements and awoke the herd.

An attack of springs approached, the elephants panicked. The disused factory began to erupt with noise! Rowan had a plan, the others ignored him because he was broken with patches sewed on, so they thought it wouldn't work.

Springs surrounded the shaking elephants until Rowan ran, the others followed him into a hot-air balloon.

It took them to a distant part of the factory. It came to a sudden halt, everyone cheered, "Rowan."

Emily Johnson (10)
Parsons Down Junior School, Thatcham

Bob's Adventure

The door slammed shut downstairs and the room came alive. Bob was fiddling about with the engine of his spaceship and it came to life.

He jumped in and went for a fly. He weaved around trees. *Smash!* He went flying into Charlie's room. Toys surrounded him and said, "Do you want us to help you rebuild your spaceship?"

"Yes please!" replied Bob. After ages of reconstruction, they finally finished it and it was twice as good as before.

He jumped in and flew back just as Harry walked into his room. "That's not where I left that!" murmured Harry.

Harrison Ord (11)
Parsons Down Junior School, Thatcham

The Creepy Doll

Once, there lived a horrible doll that went on my trampoline when I went to school. It would always go out the window to get on the trampoline. This doll was very strange because no other doll could move.

One rainy night, the doll jumped and scared my sister, the doll said, "Come play with me!"

"Argh!" shouted Rosie. Rosie booted the doll out of the window. The creepy doll wasn't seen again.

I was so scared at bedtime, I always feared the creepy doll would come back for revenge.

Bang, went the door as a wet thing walked through!

Henry Britler

Parsons Down Junior School, Thatcham

C-3PO's Mission To Mars

Lego C-3PO was bored sitting on the shelf, unwanted. Today was the day he would fly to Mars!

He hopped off the shelf and navigated through the heap of toys to the rocket. As he leapt inside, he saw his owner wake up. "Oh no, I need to get this working quickly!"

Then, the rocket took off and he found himself in the abyss of space. "Space looks like Matt's bedroom!" C-3PO pondered. He felt a burst of speed. The rocket dropped. *Boom!*

The rocket smashed to smithereens. "Oops!" cried Matt, picking up the pieces. "This took ages to build!"

Matthew Sandles
Parsons Down Junior School, Thatcham

Picnic Panic

Maileg walked dejectedly away from the riverbank where his friend Loppy had tumbled from the picnic basket into the stream. He must alert Jack to the plight of his favourite toy, but how?
With all his might, Maileg kicked an acorn. It flew straight into the back of Jack's head. "What was that?" Jack pondered. Enquiringly, he strolled towards the stream where he glimpsed a piece of grey flannel material, snagged on a thorny bush. Instantly he knew it was Loppy. "How on earth did you get here?" said Jack. "It's like you toys have a life of your own."

Jack Bartholomew (9)
Parsons Down Junior School, Thatcham

Christmas Party

At the Christmas present department, the toys were having an early Christmas party in case they got destroyed on Christmas Day.
Everyone was invited. The pandas played chess, but they blended in with the board too well. Nobody noticed that the cameras were in operation, so the security guards could see it all. They could see the stuffed teddy bears playing football, the rag dollies were doing their make-up and the toy soldiers were playing their guitars. Mr and Mrs Potato Head were putting their pieces back together from where the children had been playing about with them...

Emily Georgina Long (10)
Parsons Down Junior School, Thatcham

Operation Black Box

"We will fight on the carpet, we will fight on the fireplace, we will never surrender! And even if we get sent to the charity shop, the other toys will continue to fight against the Xbox!"

There was thunderous applause.

"This dreaded Xbox," Tank One continued, "has a hard outer shell but inside it is soft and we have the firepower to break through that hard outer shell."

All the toys applauded very loudly. "Tank Two ready. Tank Three ready. Tank Four ready. Soldiers ready. Aeroplanes ready. Ships ready. Right, let's do this. Roll out!"

William Hennah (9)

Parsons Down Junior School, Thatcham

The Great Escape

There was a beautiful toy dog called Jasper, with an evil owner, Malfoy Draco who treated him cruelly.

One day, after Malfoy had left to catch the train for a holiday, Jasper scrabbled around for Malfoy's laptop and cleverly Skyped his toy dog friend, Toby. After telling Toby how cruel Malfoy was, Toby felt a funny feeling in his tail.

Suddenly, Toby's laptop sucked him in and he burst into Jasper's house. In a flash, he grabbed Jasper and pulled him back through to his house.

Saved from Malfoy, Jasper now has a happy life with Toby and his owner.

Emily Eaves (9)

Parsons Down Junior School, Thatcham

The Plastic Prison

I awake, still trapped in my plastic prison, trying to move my arms - they are restrained. I can't reach my weapon, tied up next to me.

How long have I been here? Days turn into weeks. I strain my neck round to stare at other trapped prisoners, row upon row, all labelled in the same mysterious way. What does £9.99 mean anyway? Suddenly, a gigantic figure blocks my view, its eyes wild with excitement. "Daddy!" it cries. "I want this one!"

I am whisked away. Is this my new jailer or rescuer? I tensely await for what my future holds...

Noah Smith (10)
Parsons Down Junior School, Thatcham

It's Good To Be Square

It was very dark and he could hear sniggering.
"Look at him! He's just a square! He's got four
knobbly stubs!"
The square brick felt very upset because he was
quite useful. He'd been in a hotel, a car, a café and
a rabbit's tail!
Just because he was a square brick didn't mean he
wasn't useful. He didn't like it in this box with the
spiteful curved blocks.
Suddenly, the box lid opened and a voice
exclaimed, "I've been looking for you! I need you
for my hospital," as a hand reached in and took
him away to happiness.

Holly Kitching (10)

Parsons Down Junior School, Thatcham

Charlotte

There was once a doll named Charlotte. She used to be on every young girls' Christmas list. Parents would spend a fortune on outfits and accessories for the doll.

What really made Charlotte stand out wasn't her luscious blonde locks, her wide blue eyes or her perfectly painted teeth, Charlotte could talk.

If you were sad you'd have Charlotte. If you were angry you'd have Charlotte and if you were happy you'd have Charlotte. Overall, she would be your best friend.

However, people began to lose interest in the toy and new toys came out to replace her.

Matilda Burchett (10)

Parsons Down Junior School, Thatcham

The Bear Downstairs

Billy the teddy bear, brave and heroic, was unstoppable. After hearing a scream, our hero leapt down from his hideout and scurried across the floor, reaching his lifelong foe - stairs!
From this height, the bottom looked like a deadly abyss. Only one thing could persuade him to conquer this terror - someone in danger.
Billy grabbed a small mattress and slid down to the bottom. Looking around for the source of the screech, he saw a young boy screaming in delight over a delicious bar of chocolate.
Billy realised he had conquered his fear of the stairs for nothing.

Lauren Amelia Hatt (10)

Parsons Down Junior School, Thatcham

The Ouija Board

Once, there was a young boy called Harry Binch. He had a Ouija board. "Hello," he would say and then would go into a conversation.

Harry's friend, Caitlin, came over one day and they were talking to the Ouija board. Whilst, Harry went to get some food, Caitlin thought, *this is a good time to go to the toilet.*

Harry came back, expecting to find Caitlin and the Ouija board, but they had gone and were never seen again...

What Harry didn't tell Caitlin was that if you didn't say goodbye the board would haunt you. Goodbye!

Cydney Amelie Owen (10)
Parsons Down Junior School, Thatcham

Untitled

Once upon a time, there were four toys called Thalia, Percy, Annabeth and Grover.

One night, when Rebecca was asleep all the toys crept out of the room to explore the house.

A few minutes later, when they all got out the room, Thalia whispered to everybody, "Right, if we want to explore the house, we have to be really quiet."

Then suddenly, Grover tumbled down the stairs. Then they saw Thalia in action. She launched for the nearest toy skateboard in the house and rode as quick as lightning down the stairs. Rebecca then woke up with a start!

Rebecca P (9)
Parsons Down Junior School, Thatcham

Wasteland 2153

The year was 2153. The wasteland that remained in the aftermath of WW5 was home to an army of toy soldiers, left behind. Platoon 362 were desperately foraging for supplies when Sergeant Bob called out, "Over here!" The rest of the troop made their way over, guns in hand and stopped at the sight of an immense computer screen.

"Does it turn on?" Colonel Wilson asked. Sergeant Bob pressed the on button and the screen came to life. A huge beam of light hovered above him and before he knew it, he found himself trapped in 'Gears of War 200'.

Pierre Denis (9)

Parsons Down Junior School, Thatcham

An Adventure You Will Remember

"Argh!" Greenery spread across the vast fallen box as Bella struggled to gain consciousness. "Hello, is anybody there?" she gasped. Her fists smashed against the wooden panels.

Finally, the once sturdy walls collapsed, revealing an area of emptiness. Bella looked for every passage that could lead her to freedom.

All of a sudden, Bella heard voices saying, "Who's there?" A shocked look appeared on her face as she realised she was staring at a sea of toys.

Just then, a Jeep pulled up close to her and offered her a way out.

Charlotte Anne Carpenter (10)
Parsons Down Junior School, Thatcham

Toys 'R' Us Smackdown

At midnight, in Toys 'R' Us, WWE figures magically came to life, but moody Mark Henry wanted to ban wrestling forever! Daniel Bryan said, "If you beat me in a match you can ban wrestling forever!"
The day came for the match of a lifetime to start. The bell rang, Mark Henry ran up to Daniel and threw him out the ring! The crowd went silent. Daniel was down. The fans shouted, "Come on Daniel!"
Daniel crept into the ring. The fans cheered, Daniel took down Mark with the running knee and won the match! Daniel saved wrestling! Yes! Yes!

Curtis Haines (9)
Parsons Down Junior School, Thatcham

A New Home

The little black dog waited anxiously at the bottom of the stocking. His paws ached in the wrapping paper, he heard excited voices and tearing, his long wait would soon be over. "Oh look, there's one left at the bottom!" he heard a voice say. He felt himself being lifted up with hot hands grasping him tightly.

The paper fell away from him and he looked into the face of a happy, smiling boy. "Blackie!" the boy exclaimed delightedly. "You're just what I wanted." On the bed, the little dog saw a golden teddy smiling at him.

George Edward Keylock (9)
Parsons Down Junior School, Thatcham

Roboter The German Robot

As the van, in which Roboter was travelling to England, was about to enter the Channel Tunnel, the back door flung open. Roboter bundled out. Finally, he managed to escape the mayhem. Roboter found a car with an open window and jumped in. About halfway across the Channel, Roboter heard them speak. They were German. "Ich bin verloren," cried Roboter, (I am lost). He remembered the postcode and address, then gave it to the German family. They agreed to take him. The journey took two hours. "Danke," he said. (Thank you.)

Samuel Donegan (10)

Parsons Down Junior School, Thatcham

Monkeys In The Garden

Once, there were three monkeys that lived in my nan's greenhouse. They were my nan's garden ornaments but to me, they were my friends. When no one was looking, they came alive and we played in the garden.

We had loads of fun playing hide-and-seek and we could not stop laughing at each other. As soon as an adult came out, they stood still.

I kept on getting told off for playing with them because my nan was frightened that I would break them. I said, "I'll be careful Nan."

She said, "Yes, you will be!"

Cameron Young (11)

Parsons Down Junior School, Thatcham

The Elf's Tradition

A girl called Emma was nine years old. She lived with Mum, Dad and an older brother called Tom. It was the 30th of November. Emma wished for a Santa hat.

That night, a little red creature crept in Emma's house. On the 1st December, Emma rushed downstairs because she knew a chocolate calendar was waiting for her.

She found it but there was a creature. A note said: 'Hi I am your elf, name me'. Emma called the elf Snowflake.

They had a wonderful time. It was Christmas and Emma got her hat. Have a merry Christmas.

Esme Baron (10)
Parsons Down Junior School, Thatcham

The First Toy On The Moon

In a faraway village named Toysville, there lived an adventurous toy named Floppy. His dream? To be the first toy on the moon! After months of being told he couldn't, he finally decided it was time to do it.

He asked NASA for a rocket and set off into space. Cameras were attached to the rocket, so they could make sure he actually got to the moon. Floppy finally got there and was titled 'First Toy on the Moon'.

When Floppy was on the moon, he jumped four metres high! He got back to Toysville to celebrate his title.

Eloise Gale (10)

Parsons Down Junior School, Thatcham

Marjorie's Story

Once, a doll named Marjorie was playing with her owner, Ell. All of a sudden, Ell's mum said, "Sweetie, we've gotta go now." So they sorted every item into boxes, but the toy box was empty and Marjorie fell out! A girl named Tiffany fixed Marjorie and she had other toys to keep Marjorie happy, like Elaine the fairy and all sorts of toys to keep her company. Tiffany gave Marjorie to her sister, Cornelia, and then Marjorie saw a missing sign with her face on. She whispered to Cornelia, "I never want to come back!"

Scarlet Thompson (9)
Parsons Down Junior School, Thatcham

Phantom

In the middle of the night, electric-blue eyes pierced through my bedroom door, causing my eyesight to become blurry. A loud screeching noise filled the room, shaking a picture on the wall.
I got out of my bed, grabbing my flashlight and crept to the door. "Hello? Is anyone there?" I muttered.
My light shone on a black figure: sharp pointy ears, a long string-like tail and a small agile body! It was my teddy, Phantom, lying outside my door.
I picked Phantom up and put her on my chair as I drifted off into sleep.

Jessica Smith (10)
Parsons Down Junior School, Thatcham

Escape!

Adam's toys unfroze. Mr Ted slid off the bed and Adam's army figures gathered around the commando to hear their next mission.

The commando said, "Our mission this time is to sneak past Mum and tiptoe outside!"

Everyone cheered. The mission was on and they jumped down the cliff-like stairs. They skidded out of a gap in the wall.

They ran into the road and Mrs Mumble from the other side of the road, picked up one of them. "Oh, you might be a great present for my grandson." She waddled off.

Clara Phillips (10)
Parsons Down Junior School, Thatcham

The Invasion

"I have a plan to invade our enemies," whispered Lauren. Our enemies were one of the hardest troops to defeat, so the plan had to be good. No one knew about their mission apart from the people in the troop.

Lauren made a big speech about how they would get there and defeat them.

The next day, they set off, a group of toy soldiers ready to make their dreams happen and if it worked they would remember for a long time. They were tired of being pushed around so the plan was going to work, it had to.

Lauren Brown (10)
Parsons Down Junior School, Thatcham

The True Story Of Toy

Once, there was a boy. This boy had a toy. He didn't happen to be very imaginative so he named it, well, Toy! Toy was very plain, just a light blue gingerbread man.

The boy once went to an action park, taking Toy with him, but when they returned home Toy was nowhere to be found. All hope for Toy was soon banished to a distant memory.

Six months later, after the park had closed for winter, they went back and there on a straggly bench sat Toy just where they left him ragged, floppy and yellow with age.

Caitlin Hunt (11)

Parsons Down Junior School, Thatcham

Fudge And The Bone

Fudge was in the middle of a battle. For a small toy dog, she was tough. She had fought bellowing dinosaurs and roaring tigers to make it to the top of the stairs.

Next, she met an army of soldiers, Fudge would have to defeat them all if she was going to release the treasure being guarded. Fudge had to think quickly, what could she do?

Suddenly, she leapt into the air and with a quick grab she picked up the bone. Safely back in her bed she curled up and went back to sleep dreaming of her next adventure!

Hannah Haines (10)
Parsons Down Junior School, Thatcham

The Forgotten Toy (Fight Against People Who Don't Respect Genders)

Once in a local toy shop, a new limited edition toy was released known as 'The Eliminator'. All the boys around the area wanted to put their greasy fingers all over it.

There was only one ever sold. The child was a female. Her name was Brooklyn, she was only seven at the time. She was a quiet girl. All the boys thought she was rich. She was... by saving.

One day, she went missing, no trace. The toy collector, Brooklyn, was never seen again, nor the toy. Everyone forgot about the toy!

Arthur Pienaar (11)
Parsons Down Junior School, Thatcham

The Saviour

Once upon a toy, there was a rejected thing, Slime.
It gave disgust to adults and made kids gag.
The slime journeyed far and wide to find a place to
fit in. When it seemed hope was lost, there was an
eye-catching sign. He stared, *Toys tall, short,
beautiful and ugly.*
He approached the store. An ugly beast appeared
big and broad, he wielded an axe, but by surprise,
he was soft and nice and not big and bad.
He allowed Slime to pass. I guess you cannot judge
a book by its cover.

Morgan Galgey (10)

Parsons Down Junior School, Thatcham

Battleships

Ever wondered what your toys do when you aren't playing with them? I did, until the day I discovered the truth. The day I found my battleships coming to life was a day no one could dream of.
I walked into my room, the box was empty and they were everywhere. Most of the missiles had missed their target, I was sure Mum was going to blame me for the mess.
The red and white pegs were scattered and the ships were a mixture of fully sunk and hanging on. My room looked like a bomb had hit it!

John-Paul Perry (10)
Parsons Down Junior School, Thatcham

The Swamp Crash

"Argh!" shouted Troy. Troy's boat crashed into a tree in the swamp. "Yuck, the swamp slime is getting into my wellies. Uhhh," said Troy. "Who in the world? Wait, is that... a four-foot high frog? So slimy. Argh! Another one! Alright, I need to fix the boat and get out of here! Actually, I'll stay here and try and tame them. Wait, they have a baby, I'll fix my boat and take them with me."
Two hours later... "I've fixed the boat."

Louis Richard Lovelock (10)
Parsons Down Junior School, Thatcham

Cuddly Bear

One day, there was a cuddly toy named Biscuit. His family was his mum, Cookie; his dad, Alfie and his brother, Cyd.

One night, they went to the airport but when they got on the plane, Biscuit got lost and got on the wrong plane.

Instead of travelling to America, he ended up in Australia. He got off the plane and found he was in Australia.

Then he found out he didn't have any money to fly to America so he walked and walked until he got to America and saw his parents.

Hayden Harriss (9)
Parsons Down Junior School, Thatcham

Untitled

"Oh no guys, Jamie fell over. Let's see if he's hurt!"
When they went to see, he was screaming really
loudly, so they called the ambulance, and the
ambulance people said, "He's OK, he's just got cut
badly and has a few bruises."
They all went home with Jamie to rest. Then they
all went to their house to play with their toys.
They opened the door and saw them moving and
speaking and when they went in they saw
Jamie and he was better.

Dylan Bacchus (9)

Parsons Down Junior School, Thatcham

Mountain Bike

There was a boy, who had a favourite toy, his name was Peter and his toy was a mountain bike. You have to have a lot of accessories to become a pro. He and his friends liked going out on their mountain bikes.

One day, Peter went out on his bike and forgot his helmet. Halfway through the wood, he fell off his bike and hit his head on a tree stump and cut his head really badly.

His friend called an ambulance to come and get him. You must always wear your helmet while riding!

Tane Newton-Cook (10)

Parsons Down Junior School, Thatcham

The Final Battle

Hulk sat up at the bedroom window watching the snow fall on the ground. A large bang sounded behind him. It was Thor, his arch-enemy, throwing his hammer on the ground.

Hulk, in a fit of rage, jumped off the windowsill and threw himself at Thor, knocking him to the ground with his fists.

Suddenly, they heard footsteps running up the stairs. The bedroom door flung open and Ben, the black dog, grabbed mighty Thor by his dark red cape and dragged him to his cage of darkness...

Matthew Whatley (10)
Parsons Down Junior School, Thatcham

Quest To Climb Mount Everest

The three Lego men moved their blocky feet back and forward until they came to the base of the large white object which they called Mount Everest.
The three friends all of a sudden, spotted a large red helicopter. They ran over towards it. The friends hopped onboard, then quickly took off.
It was all going well until the engine went... *boom*, causing the friends to go flying into the air.

Owen Humphreys (10)
Parsons Down Junior School, Thatcham

Nelly The Elephant

It was Monday morning. Lucy hated Monday mornings. She slowly got up. As she did, Nelly, her toy elephant, fell out of her bed.

Once Lucy had got dressed and left her bedroom, Nelly got up and said, "Wesley, Wesley get up!" Wesley was Lucy's toy dog.

"Yes," said Wesley.

"I'm bored," sighed Nelly.

"Me too," whispered Wesley.

"Let's go on a walk," said Nelly.

"OK," shouted Wesley. Suddenly the door opened, they froze.

"Nelly, Wesley, are you having a party in here?" said Lucy. She left with her books.

"That was a close one," said Wesley.

"Yes," said Nelly.

Elsy Williams (10)
St Gabriel's School, Sandleford Priory

The Pizza Quest

"Ugh!" moaned Barbie. "I'm so bored!" Ted Bear's tummy rumbled. They were all very hungry, but then they all simultaneously had a thought... *pizza!* Optimus Prime transformed into a car and shouted, "Hop in, let's get some pizza!"
Barbie opened the door and sat down while Ted Bear clambered in. "Sweet!" Barbie exclaimed as she honked the horn!
Optimus Prime started up his engine and off they went. Over hills of stinky socks and mountains of dirty laundry, but then Optimus Prime sped up and he went faster and faster and faster
until *crash!* Looks like there's no pizza, sadly.

Millie Jones (10)
St Gabriel's School, Sandleford Priory

In Your Bed At Night

Do you ever wonder what happens in bed at night?
Do you wonder what your teddies are up to? Are
they cute and cuddly or are they old and grumpy?
We will never know... or will we?
"Eeeevvvviiieeee, come play with me."
"What's that? That's weird, it's only me and my
teddies in the house isn't it?"
Bleep, blob.
"Is that my robot? But I didn't turn it on. What's
happening?"
"I don't know."
"Who said that? This is getting stranger and
stranger. Am I dreaming? No, I can't be. I'm going
to check my teddies. Where are you? Argh!"

Evie Dancer-Bown (10)
St Gabriel's School, Sandleford Priory

The Cookies Win Again!

Slam! The front door closed. "Coast is clear," whispered the wing commander, getting up from where he'd been left. "We've got a mission, that we have failed to do for years. We need to get the cookies from their jar in the snack cupboard." The soldiers marched across the kitchen and stood in front of it. "Toy pyramid!" the commander demanded, the soldiers groaned. "We can make a start by getting to the handle!" he exclaimed. Eventually, the cupboard opened, they scrambled towards it. Suddenly, a car was heard. They froze, in awe. 16,780 attempts to get the cookies... failed!

Imogen Brown (10)
St Gabriel's School, Sandleford Priory

The Gang

It was a normal midweek morning that day, my favourite teddies were making a gang and only their friends were allowed. This meant some teddies were left out.

My favourite teddies were the ones nearest my pillow. They selected their gang members from old teddies that joined in their games. The ones left out were brand-new toys that didn't understand the bedroom rules.

One bear called Johnny became suspicious and rallied the unicorns. "Let's rip them before they rip us," he whispered.

The unicorn neighed, "What?"

"The old ones, use your horn!" A scene like no other commenced.

Eloise Taylor (10)
St Gabriel's School, Sandleford Priory

War Of The Lego People

In Eleanor's bedroom, the green and blue Lego soldiers were planning a war! The green team thought the blue team was weak.

Sergeant Minion from the blue team fed all his horses. He saw the green team in the distance, got all his horses in formation and screamed, "Charge!" and started charging.

The green team screamed, "Charge!" and started charging.

The owner came in, the toys instantly dropped to the ground and Eleanor said, "I didn't leave those there did I? I'm going to play with my soldiers every day for the rest of my life." Eleanor never regretted it.

Eleanor Bayford (9)

St Gabriel's School, Sandleford Priory

The Barbie Express

"All aboard the Barbie Express," squealed Barbie. She hopped on the train, with Ken beside her. She's always wanted to explore her house, today she was going to do it.

Chooo, chooo honked the train. First, the train went round the track at a slow pace but then it whizzed round the track out of control! Then it leapt off the track and landed on the carpet! Down the stairs, along the corridor, *bang!* Straight into the wall.

Things couldn't get worse, but then the household dog, Rover, started sniffing the train. Before they could run, Rover gobbled them up.

Madeleine Herd (10)
St Gabriel's School, Sandleford Priory

Bessy And Cloudy

When Lucy went to the shops, Bessy Bunny jumped off the bedroom table and hopped to Cloudy Dog who was sitting in a wooden chair. "Bessy," said Cloudy, "you can fly."
"How do I fly?"
Cloudy said, "Here get on the bed." So Bessy did. Cloudy sprinkled dust over Bessy. Bessy said, "Can I fly?"
"Yes!" said Cloudy.
Bessy started to get the hang of it. The breeze was cool as Bessy was flying. Then they heard footsteps so they turned into toys again. Lucy came back from the shops. "That's suspicious," said Lucy.

Zoe Toms (9)
St Gabriel's School, Sandleford Priory

Mission Is Go!

"Mission is go! Get to the sweet cupboard where the good stuff's kept. Move it!" exclaimed Sergeant, so off the soldiers went.

They parachuted down from the window, sprinted into the house, but unfortunately for them, kittens chased them out. They lost hope.

Suddenly, a human hand came swooping down and scooped them up. They entered the house, into the kitchen, then left them. When they weren't in sight they went to the sweet cupboard and tried to open it, but it was locked.

Then the boy came back and trampled on the soldiers, never to be heard from again...

Nerea Halley Martin (11)
St Gabriel's School, Sandleford Priory

The Toy Shop

Lights off, no people in sight, let's go! Suddenly, all the toys in the toy shop started to rattle and shake and all the toys were falling off shelves unexpectedly.

A massive panda teddy came tumbling down the stairs shouting, "Let's party!" so all the toys jumped out of their boxes and partied!

In the morning, the staff walked in, only to find toys scattered all round the floor and also out of their boxes!

The staff didn't know what to do, except wonder what had happened. The staff kept asking themselves, "Could the toys have come alive overnight?"

Ella Newborough (10)

St Gabriel's School, Sandleford Priory

The Wish That Came True

"I need to get out," Cow whispered to himself as he wriggled.

His wish was to reach the wardrobe to surprise Olivia by being in her pocket the next morning before school. He rolled and wriggled but whatever he did, there was always a toy or sleeping Olivia blocking his way.

Then, when he'd almost given up hope, Olivia rolled over pushing the toys onto the floor - this was his chance!

He crawled to the wardrobe and managed to open the door. He grabbed onto the sash of a dress and swing into the jumper pocket. He'd done it.
Woohoo!

Olivia Cole (10)
St Gabriel's School, Sandleford Priory

Zebby And The Pizza

Zebby was mischievous and his friends were mischievous too. One night, when the family went out, Zebby was starving. He looked in the phone book and typed 0718 07833.

He called Domino's Pizza. Zebby said, "Zghiqursa!" It means, "Give me all the pizza you have!"

Zebby waited until it came. He wrote to the pizza guy on a note, 'Put it at the back door!' Next, he went back inside with the pizza, he then heard a truck turn up and froze.

The child came in and went straight to the pizza, to eat it, Zebby was so jealous!

Ava Elverson (10)

St Gabriel's School, Sandleford Priory

How My Bed Is Made

"I want to stay home Mum," I whimpered.

"Why?" my mum said.

"I know something makes my bed, but what?" I said.

"OK, but only this once," replied Mum, so I did. I sat on the floor and waited for something to happen. Then suddenly, there was something making my bed. I crept towards it. It was Pink Bear! She was making my bed! Now I know how my bed is made when I don't do it.

She was singing and dancing. It was awesome. I went to grab her, she turned around and froze. I said, "You're alive!"

Katie-Rose Verney (10)

St Gabriel's School, Sandleford Priory

Bounce Back To Me Baby Ball

In the nursery, there was a family of eight balls. When the babies left each day, the ball family had lots of fun bouncing everywhere.

One evening, Baby Ball accidentally bounced out to the playground and spent all night in the freezing playground all alone.

The next day, two girls picked up Baby Ball and started playing with it.

One girl got excited and hit Baby Ball so hard that it smashed back through the nursery window. When Baby Ball woke up it was reunited with its family. They were so happy that they celebrated. They bounced all night long.

Neve Wright (9)

St Gabriel's School, Sandleford Priory

The Love Dog

Rebecca was sad because her boyfriend had broken up with her. She decided to go out to calm herself down.

As Rebecca left, her most favourite stuffed dog, Rose, stretched and looked around. She saw an unusual bottle, containing Rebecca's secret love potion. Everyone told her not to drink it - she did not listen to them.

The sweet-smelling potion turned her into a love dog which meant that any toy dog who saw Rose, would fall in love.

Jack Spotty Dog saw Rose and instantly fell in love! When Rebecca returned, she saw Rose had a great big smile.

Grace Lewis (9)
St Gabriel's School, Sandleford Priory

The Crazy Make-Up Doll

"I hope she has gone because I am too excited to wait to find the make-up!" said Barbra the Barbie doll. "Where does she keep her make-up?"

She opened the doors of Ellie's bathroom and was in make-up heaven. Barbra was screaming with joy - she rushed to the eyeshadow pallet and just managed to open it and smeared the eyeshadow all over her eyes.

She found a bright red lipstick and looked like a clown when she had finished. Then she went back into the bedroom shutting the heaven doors, and just in time! Ellie came in quickly.

Ellie Abbot (9)

St Gabriel's School, Sandleford Priory

Bear

I have just been replaced, me, Bear, replaced! I was the favourite toy, I had been for many years.
"What should I do?"
Owner's out. I know! "To the toy box!" Here I am... at the box. Is this a good idea? In I go, pulling gloves on my paws and a skirt around my waist. Out I come. Oh no, owner's home! Freeze! In she walks... "Silly Bear," she smiles, "how did those clothes get on you?"
Then, to my surprise, I am put on the bed! Home where I want to be. Never to be left again!

Grace Cunliffe (10)
St Gabriel's School, Sandleford Priory

Replaced

Plain Jane sat on her shelf looking down at the happy toys below. How she wished to be like them. But it could never be, for Jane wasn't beautiful, she wasn't happy and no longer the girl's favourite toy. She had been replaced. By who you ask? The china doll. The china doll was beautiful and happy. Now every night the china doll snuggled up with the girl.

One day, when the girl was out, the plain doll had had enough - she stretched out a tiny hand and pushed the china doll. She fell and smashed into sharp, ugly pieces.

Josephine Margaret Keen (11)

St Gabriel's School, Sandleford Priory

Sneaky

One evening at Christmas time, a girl named Molly was peering round an old, ancient, dusty toy shop. She searched high and low until she found a toy owl. The owl had pointy ears and red gleaming eyes, so she brought it and took it home.

Next morning, she caught the bus to school. At home, the owl was being mischievous. His red gleaming eyes had spotted her beautifully made bed. As he was cheeky he thought he would make it different.

Molly was in for a surprise when she came back. After all, the wicked owl was called 'Sneaky'.

Olivia Emily Violet (11)
St Gabriel's School, Sandleford Priory

How Does This Happen?

My doll, Maryellen, needed a fashion update, so I put purple chalk dye in her hair. When I was asleep my doll muttered, "Revenge," so she crept up into my bed and dyed my hair.

When I awoke, I looked in my mirror. My hair was green! So in retaliation, I cut my doll's fringe really short.

The next day I woke up and looked in the mirror again. My hair had been cut off! "Why?" I said. "Why did this happen?"

I glanced over at Maryellen and she seemed to have a malicious grin on her face!

Sofia Abel (10)
St Gabriel's School, Sandleford Priory

The Barbie Doll

Hi, I'm Daisy and I'm my kid's best friend. We have been together forever, I mean wherever she went I would go, like the Bahamas, Paris or Big Ben.

Then, she got a Barbie doll from her mum. Now I'm stuck in the cupboard. I have been in here for weeks now. I'm going to get revenge.

I went up the stairs and into the room. I grabbed the scissors but then the door opened... Her mum didn't see me, so I cut the Barbie's hair.

The next morning, she binned the doll and she was my kid again.

Charlotte Hamilton (11)

St Gabriel's School, Sandleford Priory

Car Chase

Favourite Teddy always played with the soldiers. One day, the soldiers said, "You need to do something for us, we've done so much for you. If you don't, we will put you in the bin."
"What do I have to do?" asked Favourite Teddy.
"You have to get us the car in the other room."
That night, when everyone was asleep, Favourite Teddy woke up and crept into the other room and found a beautiful sports car.
Favourite Teddy headed back... then a noise came and he quickly rushed!

Elspeth Mary Coughlan (9)
St Gabriel's School, Sandleford Priory

Little Leo's Luck In The Laundry

Leo was a lion with a very little body. One day, Leo got put into the laundry. The laundry was Leo's least favourite place so he wasn't very happy with Jim, his owner, for putting him in there.
First he tried to get out but suddenly he smelt his favourite food, Peperami sausage.
He crawled out of the basket and crept across to Jim's trouser pocket. He found an old Peperami sausage. It was his lucky day!
It was a good thing that Jim probably won't miss that old Peperami sausage!

Zara Taylor (9)
St Gabriel's School, Sandleford Priory

Teddy's Getaway

Old Teddy sat alone in the corner because Ismay always played with her other new toys. He thought to himself, *I should go on an adventure...*
Ismay was at school. Teddy pushed the door with all his might and crept out. When he finally got out he saw the cat, the deadly cat! He moved a bit but could not face his fears.
He ran straight back into the bedroom like a flash of lightning and shut the door tight. He thought to himself, *actually, I definitely like it in here. Phew!*

Ismay Gallup (10)
St Gabriel's School, Sandleford Priory

The Doll

No! thought Nancy the doll as I threw her in the bin. I eagerly opened my new doll, Lola.

As I went to bed that night, I saw Nancy emerge from under my bed with a hammer. She stared at me and smashed Lola.

I tried to run but all the other teddies stopped me and turned me into one of them.

I went into my cat's box and turned her into a toy and by midnight everyone was a toy just like me and you too soon! We will conquer the world and nobody will stop us. I'm coming!

Maddie Goss (10)
St Gabriel's School, Sandleford Priory

Good Or Bad Toy?

Marie had a toy called Floppsy. He got so angry because she threw her toy into the bin.

The next morning, Floppsy (the good bunny) became Bad Bunny. He recruited more toys for the job. The toys that didn't get recruited tried to protect Marie. It was war.

They set booby traps all over the house. The good toys said to the bad toys, "Meet us in the basement, we have something to show you."

The toys showed the joy of being good. The bad toys converted to their good old ways.

Gabby Thorne (10)
St Gabriel's School, Sandleford Priory

The New Toy

Wellie woke up one morning and Harry was still asleep so Wellie thought he would go back to sleep, but before he could, he noticed there was a box on the floor! He didn't care so he closed his eyes and dozed off again.

When Harry woke up, he opened it. Inside was a beautiful, toy, a girl horse. It was exactly the same as Wellie, except she was a girl and Wellie was a boy.

Then, Harry got called down to breakfast so he left the room. Then Wellie rushed off the bed to say hi. He was excited!

Mia Wright (9)

St Gabriel's School, Sandleford Priory

The Sofa

Limited edition I was, but I didn't feel like one, sat in the most dreadful corner ever. Seeing and smelling the room made my heart skip a beat.
It was just then, all my men saluted me. I knew it was time to get what we deserved. The comfy sofa. Off we marched in formation.
We came to a stop. As always, Barbie was right in the middle of the sofa. We had to make a chain. As everybody climbed we flipped over. We were on the sofa. Just then the door opened, we did it!

Charlotte Bedford (10)
St Gabriel's School, Sandleford Priory

My Old Ted

I had a teddy called Ted, original I know! It just so happens I got a new one, so I threw Ted in a box. When I was asleep, Ted jumped on my bed and ripped my new teddy. When I woke I was distraught, so Mum took me to the shop to get a new one.

The next day, he ripped it again, so I just had to have Ted. I don't trust him and I don't like him. I feel like he is always watching, waiting for the next toy to appear.

Georgia Wilson (10)

St Gabriel's School, Sandleford Priory

The Determined Teddy Bosses

One morning, Stanley the owner left home to go to school. Suddenly, all of the teddies woke up. They all shook hands to introduce themselves.

The two bosses were called Timmy and Fill. "Chop, chop, let's start searching for money," said Timmy.

"Also, let's split up to be quicker," Fill said.

"Yeah, come on, let's go!"

Off they went and searched everything except one place. "Oi Boss, we found it!"

"Yes!"

Suddenly, Stanley was there! "No, the money's gone; forever!"

Stanley locked them in a cage forever.

Thomas Colin Phillips (9)

St Paul's Catholic Primary School, Tilehurst

Money Wars

A normal day it was... until the kid vanished from the room... It was party time for toys! Then as the click of the door went... the soldier cracked a hole in the piggy bank. Obviously, the soldier did it for money.

As the soldier marched back to his house, the soldiers looked like they duplicated. Then the soldiers whispered to each other things like, "Let's play a trick on him," or, "He's not a soldier!" So they decided to lock the soldier in his house until he gave the money back. Soon he gave up and returned the money.

Daniel Sanchez Pereyra Iraola (8)
St Paul's Catholic Primary School, Tilehurst

Toys Alive

One day, there was an Xbox lying on a TV stand, but suddenly, the wire started coming out and the console said to the controller, "Come on, this is our chance to escape."

They slowly started walking towards the door. The console gently opened the door. As soon as they walked out, they saw Patrick the human. "You'll never escape," said Patrick. He picked up the Xbox and just as he was about to plug it in, the console jabbed Patrick.

There was a flash and when it was gone Patrick was the console and the console was Patrick!

Patrick McCoy (8)
St Paul's Catholic Primary School, Tilehurst

Tippytoes' Triumph

Tippytoes was a special toy, but he couldn't dance at the jungle boogie and needed to find his inner giraffe to dance with the other animals. It would be tough, so he got started.

Watching the other animals dance made Tippy cry. He wished he could join in. As the night passed, he got lonely, trying hard to dance.

Then suddenly, as the moon danced, out crawled a cricket. He couldn't hop so was sad, but that didn't stop him. Getting his courage, Tippytoes started dancing joyfully with animals whispering all around.

Lottie Mae Stretton (9)

St Paul's Catholic Primary School, Tilehurst

The Great Lime-Green Yolo!

Once, there lived a great lime-green yolo. He loved taking Snapchats of himself, he had fifteen watches and wore a different one every day. Sometimes he danced and jumped and faceplanted straight onto the pavement! He got up and ran so fast that he ran to the sea. He started swimming. Finally, he saw an island. It looked beautiful until spikes started growing! There was no way out so he used his dancing skills to chop them, then he swam until he was safe. Finally, he kept on Snapchatting and lived happily ever after!

Charley Pearson (8)
St Paul's Catholic Primary School, Tilehurst

Buster's Awesome Tour Of London

Buster was hidden in his owner's bag. He was enjoying his trip. All of a sudden, he fell out! He managed to follow them when he lost track of them! Buster tiptoed silently into the jewel house where he caught a glimpse of the jewels.

He decided, "I'd like to go to the Gherkin." He found the Gherkin and climbed up it with his laser grips. Buster eventually jumped off and landed. He zoomed back into the bag and acted as if he'd been there for the whole time.

Tom Carroll (8)

St Paul's Catholic Primary School, Tilehurst

A Bad Dream

Three soldiers woke up on a bed and then fell off.
Soldier one said, "What is happening?"
Soldier two said, "I don't know."
"Let's explore," said Soldier three.
Then they saw a train track in the middle of the
room but when they were crossing it, a train came
rushing down, knocking out the soldiers, sending
them flying. They hit the floor near the door.
Then a child squashed them under his feet and
said, "Oh that's strange!"

Michal Nowicki (9)
St Paul's Catholic Primary School, Tilehurst

The Water And Fire Ninja

Once upon a time, there was a ninja called Jake. He was the ninja of water and he was found in a very old chest.

One day he escaped and discovered a bedroom and saw a glowing spark on a table. He climbed up and saw a sword set on fire.

He picked it up and turned into water and fire. He climbed and saw an enormous baby, he tried to fight the giant baby but he got squished and died. Then a young boy turned on the light and said, "What is he doing on the floor?"

Thomas Jakes (8)
St Paul's Catholic Primary School, Tilehurst

The Toys Got Squashed

"Sergeant," said the Captain, "we have been stuck in this bed for ten days. We have to get out!"
"We can," said Sergeant, "we can climb down the bed."
"Great that's good news."
"Now, let's go down."
When they climbed down from the bed, they were squashed by their owner as they landed on the floor.
"Oh no!" said the owner. "I squashed my toys!"

Jayden Soloye (8)
St Paul's Catholic Primary School, Tilehurst

The Newest Edition Joker

"You got it?" asked Yellow.

"Yes," replied Dragon, "just let me over!"

"Not until you show us," Red said.

"Fine."

"Cool," Orange shouted.

"Shhhh," said Yellow, Red and Blue.

"Fine, you get over."

"Ouch, watch it!" Blue cried.

"Sorry," Dragon answered rudely.

On the other side of the bed, Flame Dragon met the cards who blocked his way. "You shall not pass!"

"Why?" Dragon asked.

"Not until you've become one of us," 3 of Hearts said.

"Nooo!" Dragon shouted as Ace of Diamonds tapped him with his magic stick. That's why there is a pink joker sometimes.

Tristan Meller (11)
St Peter's CE Middle School, Old Windsor

Mission Escape

"There it is," I whispered.

"Shshsh," said Koln, "let's move."

The toys followed closely.

"Argh!"

"What happened?"

"Man down," screamed Koln.

Meanwhile, Gizmo, Charlie's dog, moved on to the other troopers. "I am coming," I said.

I ran as fast as lightning to Koln. I picked him up. "Come on," shouted another trooper.

We both ran as fast as our legs could go. "Quick, get your parachutes ready!" said Koln.

Then we leapt, our parachutes making us fraught. As we got to the bottom, Daniel unhooked our parachutes and we jumped to our destination.

Joseph Rodgers (11)
St Peter's CE Middle School, Old Windsor

The Toy Cat And The Toy Mouse

"Ouch!" the mouse said to the cat. "Well, it is my job to eat you."

"Quiet Cat, I hear someone coming."

"Oh, who cares, it's probably just Bonnie."

Thud! Crash!

"What is it?"

"I don't know, there is too much smoke, I can't see anything. Help me! Help!"

"Mousey! Get back here. Mouse get back here."

"Shush Cat, we are going to Toy Land. Plus Bunnie's coming to collect us."

"But Mouse, what was that thing grabbing you?"

"Oh, that was just a prank!"

"Come on Cat and Mouse, it's time to go to Toy Land."

Kumayle Hussain (11)
St Peter's CE Middle School, Old Windsor

Battle Of Pirates

It was devastating. Blood was being shed and life lost. This was the grand finale of the pirate and robotic soldier battle.

Flimsy plastic swords were thrust into the soldiers' hyperdrives and in return, imaginary bullets embedded themselves in the pirates' legs, stomachs and heads. How much longer before this ended?

There was a small scuffle between two pirates. They disagreed with each other's strategies. "Mits up, you filthy scallywag," one exclaimed.

"Likewise, you ugly, useless wasteman," the other pirate replied, rudely.

Before they said another word, a foot crushed them. The war ended as the beast had arrived.

Camran Gangarh (11)
St Peter's CE Middle School, Old Windsor

Dawn Of The Death-Vac

"It's now or never! We have to make a run for it," shouted Slade, the Bakugan leader. The Dyson Death-Vac had turned in another direction.
This was a good opportunity to make a run through the red, woollen grasslands and reach the inter-dimensional portal. The Bakugan rouge team, Slade, Spartan, Overwatch and Arrow, assembled in escape formation and moved out.
They were making good progress when suddenly they heard a huge crashing sound. The humans had started dismantling the portal. To make things even worse, the Death-Vac was heading straight for them!
"Split up," shouted Overwatch. "It's our only chance."

Arjun Singh Kharay (10)
St Peter's CE Middle School, Old Windsor

Milo's Spooky Story

"Come on everyone, get a move on, storytime's about to begin," shouted Milo, the plush caterpillar. "Come on, Speedy the slug, get on the bed."
"Princess Unicornia, you don't always have to sit on the pillows!"
"OK, let me start," shouted Milo angrily.
"On Halloween night, Fluffy Bunny went to Bobby Bears and said, 'Trick or treat?' but Bobby Bears had run out of sweets."
Everybody looked astonished and amazed as Milo said every house had run out of candy and, with that, they all started screaming and ran to their spots and went to sleep.

Eleanor Rose Terry (10)
St Peter's CE Middle School, Old Windsor

Corkers

One night, whilst Yuri was sleeping, a snatcher took Deni (his sister) to Tokashi's lair. Tokashi was the most evil scientist in the Digiverse. He locked Deni in a cage.

When Yuri found out, he was scared and furious at the same time! He set out with his friend, Nutcracker, battling their way through the dense jungle. When they reached Tokashi's lair, they fought until Yuri used his amazing strength and Nutcracker's brilliant ingenuity to defeat him.

The Digiverse was once again safe from evil and Tokashi's parts were ground up, melted and then used to make more Corker robots.

George John Williams (11)
St Peter's CE Middle School, Old Windsor

The Midnight Adventure

It's late, Hedgehog hears a rumble and sees Bunny holding her tummy. "I'm so hungry, my tummy is rumbling! How about a midnight snack adventure?"

Hedgehog's always hungry at night so he says, "Yes please!"

"Let's go!" says Bunny.

At the stairs, Hedgehog trips and wakes the cat who, with an evil miaow, gives chase.

Bunny shouts to the cat, "If you help us, we'll help you!" The cat listens to the plan, he agrees to help them, as long as he gets a snack too.

Later, all three are moaning in pain saying, "Oh, we've eaten too many snacks!"

Charlotte Roberts (10)

St Peter's CE Middle School, Old Windsor

Bertie On An Adventure

What's happening? wondered Bertie the bunny as a strange white-bearded man in a red suit started wrapping him in paper.

He felt himself being tossed across the room and minutes later heard a cry of, "Go Rudolph!" He felt himself soaring into the air and for the next few hours felt all sorts of movements until finally, everything was quiet again.

He must have fallen asleep but was suddenly woken by a child screaming as he felt the paper being ripped from his body.

"I love you," cried the child, hugging him tightly. "You're the best Christmas present ever!"

Ayesha Scott (10)
St Peter's CE Middle School, Old Windsor

The Time War: The Daleks Fight Back

"Foy!" Foy's mum shouted at Foy for their weekend out. Foy went running out of his bedroom and the toys saw that the coast was clear.

Foy's favourite toys were his Daleks. They pushed the lid of the toy box upwards. There were 100 Daleks and 20 of them were Dalek emperors. The leaders were Dalek Supreme and Davros, the creator of the Daleks.

The toy Davros told Dalek Supreme, "You must create a spaceship and conquer the universe." The Daleks moved out of the box saying, "Exterminate, exterminate." Then the other toys surrendered. The Daleks were just too powerful.

Nihal Bath (10)

St Peter's CE Middle School, Old Windsor

Toys At Night

Bella is tired of shelf life. "Get up, get out of bed!" she shouts.
The still darkness explodes with singing, popping, roaring, banging and clashing. Lights flash like fireworks. Bella stares in disbelief. Cars are zooming round the floor, aeroplanes flying, soldiers marching, robots chanting, dolls skipping, puppets acting, trains hooting, all happy to be alive! "What a great way to spend the night, but how am I going to get them back to bed?" worries Bella. She spies a drummer boy. A thundering drum roll stops the toys in their tracks. Bella sighs. All is quiet until next time.

Georgia Harradine Quarteman (10)
St Peter's CE Middle School, Old Windsor

The Courageous General

As soon as the family left the house, General immediately told his soldiers to patrol in a defensive circle around their base (the boy's bed) to protect them from attack.

Unlike some generals, who stay back from the fight, General was always in the heat of the battle. He loved gunfire.

"We're under attack!" a scout warned urgently.

General ordered his men to attack the oncoming soldiers. They were so fierce that the attackers almost immediately retreated.

General ordered his army to pursue the fleeing soldiers. He was not going to put up with this. "Attack!"

Isaac Gadsby-Gower (10)

St Peter's CE Middle School, Old Windsor

The Runaway Toys

"This is our chance," whispered Mippy, "let's go!"
They ran out of the door then followed the path.

"Are you sure this is the way?" worried Mephany
as he took another step.

"Uh-oh," screamed Mippy.

There in front of them was Prince, the bulldog. He
was the toughest dog in history.

As soon as Mephany saw him, he screamed. That
caught Prince's attention so he started chasing
them to a dead end, Mippy and Mephany were
trapped.

Then suddenly, Mippy woke up from a bad
nightmare and saw Mephany was safe in bed,
snoring away with Tom.

Lauren Tullett (10)
St Peter's CE Middle School, Old Windsor

Being Zebiong

Zebiong was a friendly toy alien with a personality like no other. But on one tragic day, he and Kile (his best friend) ventured too close to the stairs and then Zebiong slipped and fell.

When Zebiong woke, he felt a soggy liquid slipping swiftly across his face. "That's disgusting," he said. He opened his eyes and saw slobber from the monster, but he wasn't scared. He'd had lessons in martial arts.

Without hesitation, he karate chopped its nose and sat between its eyes to ride it all the way upstairs. When he got there they were ferociously shivering.

Thomas Butler (10)
St Peter's CE Middle School, Old Windsor

Zid And Zod's Pranks

Zid and Zod were two aliens who loved to mess with humans and make them think they're going crazy.

"Hey Zod, let's make the humans think we are moving around." Zod thought this was a great idea so when a little boy came home from school, Zid and Zod started to wiggle around and when the boys' parents came in they instantly froze.

When the boy went out of his room, Zid and Zod were laughing so much they couldn't control themselves.

"Zid that was the best idea you've had yet!"

"Next time it'll be an even better prank!"

Angel Richards (10)

St Peter's CE Middle School, Old Windsor

The Great Rescue

"Dave, I have looked, the shop opens at 9am. We can escape at 8am tomorrow because the shopkeeper comes in at 8am and leaves the door open."
"It's time to go!" Dave the dog said, "but where is Jeff the Joker? We need to search for him."
"But we have to leave."
"No, we are not going without him."
"Hey, I've found him."
"But, it is 10am, it's too late!"
"No, we have to go today, we can finally escape."
"Oh, but there is another toy coming in. We need to save him!"

Thomas Mullan-Smith (11)
St Peter's CE Middle School, Old Windsor

Pipi The Penguin And The Great Adventure

"It's time for another adventure!" exclaimed Pipi, as he jumped off the bed. The other toys looked at him, annoyed because he'd woken them up.

Pipi's friend, Lita the ladybird said, "What a way to wake up! A penguin screaming out loud like there is nobody in this house."

"Sorry," muttered Pipi, climbing on to the bedside table. He gasped as he saw something between the bed and the bedside table which made him fall into the gap!

"Oh no Pipi, what have you done now?" said Rachel as she walked into her bedroom and gave him a big hug.

Maham Omar Mirza (10)
St Peter's CE Middle School, Old Windsor

The Forgotten Toy

"Shhh," I heard the boys say. My heart was pounding. I had a feeling of excitement. Would they find me at last? My rusty arms started to feel much stronger, I could move them again.

The squeaky cupboard door finally opened for the first time in two years. "What's this?" I heard Harvey say to his friend.

"I've been found at last," I said to myself, "hooray!"

Harvey carefully grabbed me out of the cupboard. He ran downstairs to get some batteries. At last, this old forgotten robot will finally be played with again! "Yippee!"

Jack Hollick (10)

St Peter's CE Middle School, Old Windsor

Mr And Mrs Salt And Vinegar Battle On

"Help, help, I'm drowning," cried Mrs Salt.
"Don't worry, I'll save you," shouted Tommy Ketchup!
Tommy runs as fast as he can to the water but he falls splat on his face in the sand. Poor Mrs Salt, what will she do? "Not to worry," calls Colonel Mustard, "I'll rescue you. I'll jump in my banana boat, not forgetting my bagel ring."
Colonel Mustard throws the bagel ring and Mrs Salt catches the bagel ring and Colonel Mustard pulls her to the sand and they all have a party, leaving Tommy Ketchup lying flat on the floor!

Jaye Long (11)
St Peter's CE Middle School, Old Windsor

The Lost Jessie

"What are we going to do?" said Woody. "We're trapped and Jessie's lost!" Woody was worried, he didn't know what to do.

"Don't worry," said soldier one, "we'll find her and when we do, we'll be free."

Then they heard a sound so they all ran to hide. Then out of nowhere, there was Jessie.

Everyone was grateful except Lots-a-Legs, he was always moody even when he got what he wanted. Finally, an hour later they were free. The doors opened and they ran. They were delighted but where had Jessie gone again?

Eisha Darcia (10)

St Peter's CE Middle School, Old Windsor

The Escapades Of Maisy And Bertie

Up on the shelf, far from harm, sat Maisy. Maisy was a rag doll, a very upset doll at that. For Maisy, our heroine, longed for adventure, battles with pirates and finding treasure but how could she travel the world when she was sat on a shelf? "A few more," Maisy muttered to her best friend, Bertie Bear. Bertie Bear put more building blocks on the pile. "Perfect!" whispered Maisy as she climbed down next to Bertie.
"I didn't think we would make it," mused Bertie. With that, they snuck out of the bedroom. They were off to find adventure!

Freya Holden-MacDonald (11)
St Peter's CE Middle School, Old Windsor

The Invasion

"Get to our secret bunker," shouted Bob, as they ran to their secret bunker bombs started going off and smoke grenades were being thrown.

"Get down," screamed Dave.

They all had to stay still. Their enemy was coming through the bushes. "What are we going to do?" asked Sal.

As the enemy got closer, the good guys put up their weapons and fired! As the enemy's bodyguard died, a sniper shot the leader. When the leader died, all the others ran!

"Owww!" screamed Jeff. He looked down and saw lots of mini figures on the floor.

Charlie McCreanor (10)
St Peter's CE Middle School, Old Windsor

Untitled

Once upon a time, there was a boy called Finnley.
He went to school and said, "Where are my
friends? They've got to be here somewhere."
Then it was home time so he walked home and
said, "Hi Mum."
Mum said, "What is the matter?"
"My friends are gone. I am going to my room."
He opened his door, sat on his bed and looked at
his toys and said, "My friends are right in front of
me, I must tell Mum!"
Then Mum walked in and saw him talking to them.
"So you found them."
"Yes, Mum."

Finnley Viotto (10)
St Peter's CE Middle School, Old Windsor

Twin Teddies

Once upon a toy, there lived two teddies named Lolly and Pop, they were twins. Lolly was pink and Pop was purple.

One day, they were walking through Gummy Bear Forest when wind came and Pop fell into Candy Brook! "Help, help!" she cried.

"Here!" Lolly replied. She pulled out her bright rucksack and found a superhero outfit with a rope inside.

She quickly slipped the outfit on, grabbed the rope and flung it into Candy Brook for Pop to hold. Pop held the rope tightly whilst Lolly pulled her out. From now on, Pop calls Lolly Super Lolly!

Poppy Jane Alden (10)
St Peter's CE Middle School, Old Windsor

The Dance-Off

"I'm prepared, let's go," said the Nutcracker. Everyone from his house followed him across the blue carpet then onto the pink. Now they knew they were in their enemies' territory.

They waited. Suddenly the Pinks came out of their doll's house. After two minutes, the leader of the Pinks pressed a button on the boombox and started dancing.

The Nutcracker was confused, but danced anyway. Right then the Blues realised it was a dance-off, between the house leaders.

At the end of the dance-off there was a cheer from the winning dance team!

Rebecca Barrack (11)
St Peter's CE Middle School, Old Windsor

Toy Twins

There were two twin toys called Milly and Molly.
One day, they realised they had something special.
When Milly was sad, Molly would know and when
Molly was happy, Milly would know.
Milly went for a walk by the river with their dog,
Jasper. She chucked a branch in for Jasper and lost
her step falling into deep water. Struggling to
catch her breath, she was drowning and nobody
was around to help!
Molly suddenly appeared running down the
riverbank! Molly pulled Milly to safety with a big
stick! Molly hugged Milly so tight. "Thank God, I
just knew!"

Ellie-Mae Brazier (10)
St Peter's CE Middle School, Old Windsor

The Christmas Tree Candy Cane Mystery

It was a dark night. Ellie and her parents went to bed. On Christmas Eve, on the tree, hung two wooden toys, a soldier and a ballerina.

Once Ellie was gone, they woke up! "Time for Operation Candy Pain Spies," said Grace, the ballerina.

"No!" said Jack. "It's Candy Cane."

All of the candy canes on the tree were broken! As quick as a flash Grace and Jack mended the candy canes!

It became dawn, they were fast asleep when Ellie came down but there was one candy cane still broken. Ellie saw it, smiled and ran off.

Evie Lewis (10)

St Peter's CE Middle School, Old Windsor

Untitled

Incredibly, whilst walking in wonderful Windsor, Blue Panther saw the truck of his dreams. The truck 'Blue Phantom' was parked with a 'For Sale' sign.

He brought the truck, but as he was driving it away, a bad-looking man ran out of Lloyds Bank. Blue Panther saw the bank manager running after him.

Blue Panther drove his truck in front of the baddy and stopped him. Blue Panther was a hero.

The Queen invited him to Buckingham Palace for tea. Lloyds Bank gave him a reward. Blue Panther was pleased with the truck and went home and washed it.

Archie Padwick (10)
St Peter's CE Middle School, Old Windsor

The Ultimate Party!

At Party Palace, BFB was doing some of his best backflips ever, until FFF came in with some sweet front flips, but BFB wasn't about to let FFF take over Party Palace.

BFB decided to search for his dad's awesome book of flips, backflips, front flips and side slips, but didn't know where it was kept until he thought to ask his grandfather.

He told BFB it was in the one place BFB hadn't looked; the forbidden chest. So BFB opened the chest and quickly learnt all flips so he challenged FFF to a contest, then claimed back Party Palace.

Marcus Barron Cheeseman (10)

St Peter's CE Middle School, Old Windsor

Lost In The Toy Store

It was a special day when a special unicorn got delivered to a toy store. Her name was Rose-Gold. The toy store's owner's daughter named the stuffed animal Rose-Gold. Rose-Gold's nickname was Rose.

Rose was the only unicorn in the toy store so she made friends with some other unique toys like mermaids, fairies and pink elves.

They got lost in the toy store a lot because it was a gigantic shop. They always found their way out. One sunny day Rose and her friend got bought by a little girl called Sophia. They stayed with her forever.

Simone Williams (10)
St Peter's CE Middle School, Old Windsor

The Day The Toys Talked Back

"I wish I was a toy!" exclaimed Zach. He collapsed. He woke up with huge toy people around him. "Who are you?" asked Zach. "Where am I?" The toys spoke back, "You're in Toytopia! We found you lying on the beach, we suspected that you got washed up on the shore but we are not sure how you got here."

Zach didn't like it here, he thought all the toys were a bit creepy. He saw a few toys: Lego, PlayMobile and a few chess pieces. They did look very scary! He made his way through the forest to home.

Max Kaczmarczyk (10)
St Peter's CE Middle School, Old Windsor

The Mysterious Mini Figures

Every night I would put my Lego mini figures away in my favourite storage box. I would wake up every night to a distant noise in the background.
It was almost like my mini figures came to life at night while I was sleeping. However, that can't be true as it's just Lego.
I would wake up every morning to my Lego storage box wide open with all my Lego figures laid out on my bedroom floor.
I explained to my mum what was happening with my Lego. She laughed and said, "Well that's mysterious, maybe they awoke at night!"

Jason Finlayson (10)
St Peter's CE Middle School, Old Windsor

Woody And The Toys 'R' Us Adventure

Ding-dong, ding-dong chimed the clock, it was midnight! Suddenly, Woody started moving and then all the other toys punched open their wrapping and jumped off the shelves.

The army soldier formed an arrowhead and Woody and the others formed a line. The head army soldier walked into the middle of the room and so did Woody. They shook hands and said, "Let the games begin!"

The army soldiers were shooting their guns, when suddenly, the lights turned on and a boy walked in, he saw the mess and said, "Where's Woody?"

Ben Corrigan (10)
St Peter's CE Middle School, Old Windsor

The Toy Off The Shelf

One lonely Monday, a toy on a shelf got knocked down, nobody picked him up. When lights went out, he got up and started trying to get back but couldn't.

He found his friend. He said, "Can you help me to my shelf?" He got other toys to help but couldn't get up. He kept trying, everyone left because the lights were turning on.

He hid in the storage room but got lost in there. He was between loads of boxes and men that couldn't see him. He was trying to get attention but couldn't. He was lost and forgotten.

Ethan Wood (10)

St Peter's CE Middle School, Old Windsor

Robot Robert And The Shutters

9pm struck just as the shutters were going down, the vibration made Robot Robert fall off the shelf. He hit the wall and turned on. Slowly, Robert stood up and started throwing toys around the store! 6am the next morning, the store opened as the manager walked in grumpily.

He saw that somebody had been in the store! He immediately called the police. They scanned the items and said that the fingerprints were plastic! They saw they were Robert's and turned him off for good. They also took the batteries out so he could not work at all!

Scarlett Breach (10)

St Peter's CE Middle School, Old Windsor

Bob

I'm Bob, Pops' favourite teddy. We love playing in the park and spend every second together in the playground. Our favourite thing is climbing trees. As Pops jumped down from the tree, she couldn't find me. She looked high and low. Her cruel mum shoved her in the car and drove off.
I stood up alone and cried. Then I rolled down the tree and left the park.
Our local bus was passing, luckily I jumped on until we passed our house. Then I climbed up the drainpipe, went through the open window to cuddle my beautiful Pops.

Millie Edwards (10)
St Peter's CE Middle School, Old Windsor

Ted's Adventure

As the present got unwrapped, a big smile grew on Sarah's face. "A teddy, I'm going to call him Ted," she said happily.

That night, Ted was kept cosy in a nice warm bed. The next day Sarah and Ted went to the park, it was autumn so the trees looked beautiful.

Both of them played on the swings and slides. Sarah's mum asked her to look at something but she did not come back!

Days, hours and minutes passed. Ted was asleep but was soon awoken by Sarah! He was so happy to have his best friend back!

Hannah Rowley (11)
St Peter's CE Middle School, Old Windsor

The Party

"Go, go, go!" I hear someone shout as Lily walks off. We're having a party because it's our 5th anniversary since Lily got us. She loves Lego and this year I'm doing the lights.

"OK Mark, what do I have to do?' He explains the switches and goes to break. I press a red button and all the lights go out. "Oh no," I say.

I run to the fuse box but I need a spare piece so I get one from the spare pieces.

Everyone is angry at me. I quickly put the piece in. "Oh no, Lily!"

Jasjotika Singh (10)
St Peter's CE Middle School, Old Windsor

Mr Piggy Has A New Friend

Once, there was a piggy called Ryan. He was fast asleep. Suddenly, somebody woke him up. He was all gloomy but when he opened the curtains, the birds were twittering loudly in the trees.

He started to get dressed into his normal T-shirt, trousers, socks and shoes. He ate breakfast and found his keys and unlocked the door and by accident, fell down the stairs.

Someone helped him up and Ryan asked, "Do you want a drink?"

He said, "Yes."

After that, they went to the park. They became best friends.

Riley Moule-Wood (11)
St Peter's CE Middle School, Old Windsor

A Day At Preschool

Hi, I'm Ben and today I'm a bug and my sister, Bella, is a cat. We're Bunchems and Tom, our owner, has brought us to preschool. "What's that noise? It sounds like a bell."
Suddenly, lots of children are swarming around us. I'm thrown on the ground by a little boy and Bella is pulled to pieces by two children fighting over her. I can't reach her and it makes me sad.
I wish Bella and I were back in Tom's house again, stuck together in the shape of a dinosaur, safe on the bookshelf.

Hannah Evans (10)
St Peter's CE Middle School, Old Windsor

The Great Battle (Human Vs Toy)

Today was the very first day the human discovered we could move by ourselves. He threw Bouncer to the ground. Bob the lizard fought back and slapped the human on the leg, which caused the human immense pain and he fell to the ground crying.

We all went back where we originally were. The mum came in the room and asked the boy what happened. The boy replied, "The toys attacked me!"

The mum didn't believe him and put a plaster on each toe because he often scraped his knees.

Then, all the lizards attacked!

Adam Elliott (10)

St Peter's CE Middle School, Old Windsor

Untitled

In a happy home lived a curious gang of toys, one of which was called Flutterby. She was a fairy doll and was treated like a queen by her child and toy friends.

It was a cold winter's day and Lucy (her child) took her on holiday but Flutterby was left in the hotel room!

When the toys found out, they were super angry! They found the address and set off to rescue her! They crossed busy roads and travelled over vast fields and finally found the hotel. Slowly they snuck inside, there she was, safe and sound!

Jessica Tambling (10)
St Peter's CE Middle School, Old Windsor

The Teddy Who Needed Love

Once, there lived a teddy who lived on a shelf. Everyone around him was the exact same and every day a girl or boy would come and choose a bear.

He had never been picked. The teddy had wanted to be loved by a little child but he sometimes thought it would never happen.

One day he woke up to find himself in a bin, he started to cry, "Why would they abandon me?" Suddenly, he heard a cheerful laugh. He looked around to see a small child running towards him. The child picked him up and hugged him.

Olivia Rigby (11)
St Peter's CE Middle School, Old Windsor

Moppet's Sea Life Adventure

It was a hot, sunny day, so my family and I decided to go to the beach. I took my black and white toy cat, Moppet, with me to splash in the waves. Suddenly, Moppet's paw slipped out of my hand and she floated off into the English Channel! I ran back to my mum and dad who called the coastguard.

Moments later, a massive helicopter swooped over our heads and flew off into the distance. They were gone for hours but just as I was giving up hope the helicopter returned and a kind lady delivered Moppet safely home.

Holly Alden (10)

St Peter's CE Middle School, Old Windsor

Barry The Amazing Bear

One day Barry Bear was in the town and he saw some wonderful flowers for Auntie, so to save up the money, he washed windows.

The next day, he went back and bought them. The shopkeeper thought he stole them and called the police.

Barry got sent to jail. The food in jail was disgusting so he taught the chef to make strawberry jam sandwiches. Everybody thought he was such a good cook, they let him go.

To celebrate, Auntie Vienna threw a party for Barry when he got home, he gave her the flowers.

Alaina Howard (11)
St Peter's CE Middle School, Old Windsor

The Toy Adventure

Once upon a time there was a toy called Squish. Not many people liked him but they liked Stick next to him.

One day, he went on an adventure around Toys 'R' Us because he wondered why people didn't like him. He was walking around when the other toys were sleeping.

He got to the warehouse and there were no squishes so he walked to the toilets and looked in the mirror and he said, "Who is that?"

He got Barbie to put make-up on him, then lots of people bought him and he was happy.

Harvey Keegan (11)
St Peter's CE Middle School, Old Windsor

Jelly The Bath Toy Whale

Jelly was sitting in the toy shop, amongst all the other bath toys, when along came a boy and his mum.

He searched through the toys and pulled out Jelly. "Please can I buy him?" he asked. His mum agreed and they went to the till.

Jelly was stuffed into a bag and put in their car. He was going to his new home. There was a sudden jolt and off they went.

It was only a short journey and soon ended with yet another sudden jolt. Jelly had arrived at his new home - his dream had come true. Yay!

Eve Jarvis (10)
St Peter's CE Middle School, Old Windsor

The Mermaid's Wish Came True, But...

Once, there was a mermaid called Rose. She wanted to be a human, living in the fresh air.
As she was swimming, she saw a wish tree. She saw many wishes. She wanted to make a wish, so she closed her eyes and said, "I wish I could be a human."
Then, when she went home to sleep, she felt something weird going on. She was a human! She swam to the surface for air.
She got clothes and went to the city to see what it was like. She saw many things but she disappeared. Nobody saw her again.

Amanda Kyla Valenzuela (10)
St Peter's CE Middle School, Old Windsor

Leo's Birthday

It was Leo's birthday and he was sitting in his armchair in the dark. Jumbo wanted to say happy birthday to his friend, but when he got to Leo's house, it was dark inside.

Jumbo didn't want his friend to be sad so he decided to make a cake. He went to Linnie's shop and bought the items.

At home, Jumbo made a fine cake. It was soft, fluffy and colourful.

He took it to Leo's house and they ate it together. In the end, Leo had a great birthday with his best friend, Jumbo.

Grace Bennett (11)
St Peter's CE Middle School, Old Windsor

From Trash To The Track!

Rob, the toy car, was lonely. He was broken and only had three wheels, he sat in the clearance section for fifty pence.

I was browsing in the shop and found Rob. There was something special about him, so I took my money, paid for him and rushed home.

When I got home, I got out my tools and spare toy car wheels. I gave Rob some lovely new wheels and a paint job.

Later that day, Rob looked like a brand-new car. Rob was now a proud racing car far from the clearance section of the toy shop.

Charlie Field (10)

St Peter's CE Middle School, Old Windsor

The Love Pencil

As you know, we use pencils for drawing and writing. All pencils start off tall, then get shorter. One tall pencil was bought by a little girl, she used him for drawing. Every day he got smaller.
One day, he fell out her bag. Soon after that, a man picked the pencil up and gave it to his son. Before the pencil was too small to use, his last act was to write a love letter to the girl he was first with. The son and the little girl fell in love after the small love letter.

Danny Dick (10)

St Peter's CE Middle School, Old Windsor

The Poor Girl And The Turtle That Speaks

There was a girl called Renata Hikura, she was mature and she lived alone in the lost village.
No one liked her, but one day, she found a turtle. The turtle could talk and now she remembered that she read in 1983, someone saw a turtle that could talk, but the person had a problem in his head.
They became friends and found a secret place to stay and play!
Renata grew up but the turtle didn't. She realised that it was a toy. She had a daughter and gave the turtle to her.

Sara Renata Espinosa (10)
St Peter's CE Middle School, Old Windsor

Polly And Olivia's Story

One lovely day in London, a little girl named Olivia went to a small toy shop.

Smiling happily, she bought a teddy penguin. The penguin had a blue bow and a blue scarf. The little girl adored her penguin. Olivia named her penguin Polly. Olivia played with her toy every day.

As she grew older, Polly was forgotten. She was all on her own on the shelf.

Polly was extremely sad. She got very angry. She went red. Polly got furious, she had a plan! She was going to get her back!

Jessica Davies (10)
St Peter's CE Middle School, Old Windsor

The World Outside A Bedroom

Hi, I'm Boby and I live in a room. I'd never been out of it so I decided to go on a little adventure.

I set off and creaked open the door and popped out. I slid down the stairs into the sitting room and I saw a massive screen.

I sat there and wondered what it was. Then it started moving and glowing and I got scared and ran out.

Then a lady came and said, "Sam must have left it on so I'll turn it off." Boby never knew the mystery of the screen.

Zaki Sfendla (10)
St Peter's CE Middle School, Old Windsor

The Lost Toy

A little car named Billy fell from the shelves and couldn't get back because he was a top shelf toy. People started walking in and he had to hide. It turned night-time and no one was in the shop so he tried getting back to his shelf.

A few hours later a boy found Billy the racing car and he asked his mother if he could get it and she said yes.

Billy saw the other toys and he was so happy that he was bought. The little boy was happy that he picked the last car.

Ryan Wood (10)
St Peter's CE Middle School, Old Windsor

Sparkles The Unicorn

Hi, I'm Sparkles, I'm glittery, pink and rainbow coloured. I used to be really famous. Other toys told me I was a trend.

Then a girl called Emma bought me. We were BFFs but then I was thrown out. Emma was too old so I went to charity.

Then a girl about 17 found me and rebuilt me and then people loved me.

I was boxed up and bought from Toys 'R' Us and the girl who bought me looked like Emma. I was famous and was a new trend.

Jerusha Jayasingh (10)
St Peter's CE Middle School, Old Windsor

Untitled

One day, the toys were in a forest called Mount Toyer. There were many toys but the thing they were looking for was the treasure. It was in the cave of Skully Dragon.

They went in and there was the dragon. It was black, gold and silver. The toys searched for a minute.

Then they saw a glowing orb but it wasn't the treasure they thought it was. It was an orb of power. At least it was a souvenir, so they got some power and ran out of the cave.

Billy Palin (10)

St Peter's CE Middle School, Old Windsor

The Last Hope

On a sunny day, Mim was on a hot and big beach when he saw a star up in the sky.

When the star crashed, he saw a magic potion and drank it without thinking. He turned small with the power of wind.

Suddenly he saw a bad guy called Sam. He went to blow him up but when he got there the bad guy zapped him with his powers. Then Mim used his powers again but so did Sam.

There was an explosion and Sam was knocked out and Mim won!

Ethan Lee (10)

St Peter's CE Middle School, Old Windsor

The Guild Of Drezingtabol

The soldiers were afraid. They were the Guild of Drezingtabol attacking the feared armies of Wor'Dobe. Angus padded silently past the Zgertin Bord and the chair.

He and RoarEe hijacked a drone and flew up to the bookshelf. They landed near the midnight gang. Epic!

Angus and RoarEe dispersed. RoarEe ran along the Gartan Royle whilst Angus climbed the water pipes. He froze.

Commander Banjimon made the signal, RoarEe and Angus pulled out their fifty calibre rifles and they...

"Charlie!" Mum called. "Dinner!"

"Aw Mum!" Charlie called back, "Angus and RoarEe were just about to blow up the Lego!"

Charlie Fogg (9)
Thorngrove School, Highclere

The Infinite March

"Forward march! Here comes the hill."

"Commander?"

"What, soldier?"

"Man down."

"Drag him up the hill!"

This is the only hill that no one has climbed up.

Once the trooper was dragged up the hill, they carried on their march. They walked and walked and walked. Then a trooper asked if they had actually moved. The commander replied, "Of course."

Then a shadow fell over the troops and a voice said, "Fred, why are your soldiers on the treadmill?"

Gus Murray (10)

Thorngrove School, Highclere

The Cheeky Monkeys

Hello, my name is Tim and I'm a monkey. I have two brothers and my mum and dad. It was night and my brothers and I went to the other side of the jungle to play hide-and-seek.

Then I saw a fierce creature with sharp claws and big pointy teeth. We quickly climbed up a tree, then the horrible creature came out of the shadows and said, "Can I play?"

I was shaking, then we said, "Yes."

It was fun playing hide-and-seek, but we said we needed to get back before it was morning.

Chloe Shore (9)
Thorngrove School, Highclere

The Stolen Robots

I woke to a hard feeling under me. I have three robots and I love them! I always sleep with them. I quickly jumped out of my bed and ran down the stairs.

Ten minutes later, they were gone! I frantically searched for them but they were nowhere to be seen.

Suddenly, I saw a ghost. It had black skin and two white eyes. I was too scared to scream! The only thing that came out was a shaky, "Hi."

Suddenly, the floor under me broke through and I fell down, down, down. Soon I was gone.

Setareh Elvinna Garett (9)

Thorngrove School, Highclere

The Little China Doll

I was so sad in that charity shop, no one wanted to buy me. No children came in and looked at me until one day, a little girl came in and saw me. She went over and picked me up and she called to her granny, "Can we get this doll? It's only 25p" Her granny said, "Yes," and she gave the shop owner some pennies.

It was a long and breezy walk home but I was grateful to have a home. When we got home, she took me to play happily, she cleaned me up and we played.

Eleni Gomez (9)
Thorngrove School, Highclere

Lego Explosion

In a box full of Lego lived some lovely friends. They were very happy. Nobody bought them so every year they rejoiced!
One Saturday, they weren't so lucky, they got taken away by a kind little girl. "Why are we moving?" asked Olivia, one of the friends.
"We must've been bought," replied her friend, Mia. "When she opens the box, run."
"OK," replied the others.
"She's opening the box, run!" demanded Mia.
But the little girl didn't mind, she let them run. Before they went she said, "Be my friends." So the toys befriended the kind little girl.

Qiu Qiu Wei (9)
Waverley School, Finchampstead

The Little Unicorn

The toy unicorn jumped out of the toy box and landed lightly on the carpet. "I feel like doing some exploring, but where should I go?" she asked herself. She paced along the carpet whilst scanning the area.

The unicorn found a small cupboard right next to the door. She peered inside. "Perfect!" she squealed and trotted gaily into the closet.

Suddenly, the door snapped shut behind her. She was trapped!

A few minutes later, a girl came in. She walked to the closet and opened it to choose some clothes. She found the unicorn and played with it instead!

Margaret Samuella Oppong-Mensah (9)
Waverley School, Finchampstead

The Magic Ring

This ring that I got given for my birthday, guess what? It's magical! Whenever I put it on, it turns me into a beautiful mermaid!

My mum and dad don't know what it does because I turn into a mermaid at night.

I go out to our pod then... *poof!* I'm in the sea. I meet all my friends! Shh! Don't tell my mum and dad, it's a secret!

Oh, I forgot to mention, don't tell anyone you know except your best friends! It's completely beautiful because it's made of beauty and beauty is my thing! So weird!

Olivia Woolger (9)
Waverley School, Finchampstead

The Flower And Her Friend

There once was a flower. She had pink petals. One day her flowerpot was broken. She was free! She could walk so she walked around and suddenly she realised she lived in a giant house!

Then she realised there was a pea hiding in the corner. The flower asked the pea, "Are you OK? Do you wanna be my friend?"

The pea said, "Yes, I'm OK and yes I do wanna be your friend." It was night so they went to bed.

Next day they went out and suddenly a person came out and squashed them, so they were dead.

Keira Di Rocco (9)
Waverley School, Finchampstead

Est.1991

YOUNG WRITERS INFORMATION

We hope you have enjoyed reading this book – and that you will continue to in the coming years.

If you're a young writer who enjoys reading and creative writing, or the parent of an enthusiastic poet or story writer, do visit our website **www.youngwriters.co.uk**. Here you will find free competitions, workshops and games, as well as recommended reads, a poetry glossary and our blog.

If you would like to order further copies of this book, or any of our other titles, then please give us a call or visit **www.youngwriters.co.uk**.

Young Writers
Remus House
Coltsfoot Drive
Peterborough
PE2 9BF
(01733) 890066 / 898110
info@youngwriters.co.uk

 @YoungWritersUK    @YoungWritersCW